COLONEL ZOO

Translated from the French by
•••••••••••••••••••••••••••••••Cole Swensen

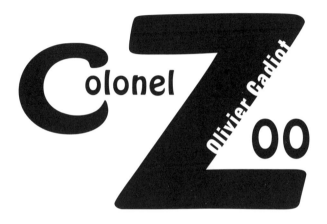

Colonel Zoo

Olivier Cadiot

1 ⋆ Masterworks of Fiction (1997)

GREEN INTEGER
KØBENHAVN & LOS ANGELES
2006

GREEN INTEGER BOOKS
Edited by Per Bregne
København / Los Angeles

Distributed in the United States by Consortium Book
Sales and Distribution, 1045 Westgate Drive, Suite 90
Saint Paul, Minnesota 55114-1065
Distributed in England and Europe by
Turnaround Publisher Services
Unit 3, Olympia Trading Estate
Coburg Road, Wood Green, London N22 6TZ
44 (0)20 88293009

(323) 857-1115 / http://www.greeninteger.com
Green Integer
6022 Wilshire Boulevard, Suite 200A
Los Angeles, California 90036 USA

First Green Integer Edition 2006
This book was first published as *Le Colonel
des Zouaves* (Paris: P.O.L., 1997)
French edition copyright ©1997 by P.O.L éditeur
English language edition copyright ©2006 by Cole Swensen

Design: Per Bregne
Typography: Kim Silva
Cover photograph: Olivier Cadiot by permission of P.O.L
The author would like to thank Marion Schoevaert
for her help with this translation.

LIBRARY OF CONGRESS CATALOGING IN PUBLICATION DATA
Cadiot, Olivier [1956]
Colonel Zoo
ISBN: 1-933382-54-6
p. cm – Green Integer 135
I. Title II. Series III. Translator

Green Integer books are published for Douglas Messerli

*Curious / it's not a rose I touch /
it's always you*

1

The drive begins at the wrought-iron gates and winds on through the shadows for several miles. If it weren't for the fields opening out suddenly from time to time between the walls of black cedar, you'd think you were heading underground. After countless turnings, the dark tunnel ends in a grey brick Tudor facade punctuated with mullioned Elizabethan windows all bearing armorial shields.

Rounding an arc of the perfect circle with a light crunching of gravel, which is raked twice a day *you shave how many times a day? Twice, you say? Be as good to the rest of the world as you are to yourself, OK,* the Aston Db4–sixteen coats of deep marine paint–stops in front of the double curved stairway. A tall, elegant man, impeccably turned out in ostrich-skin driving shoes, jodhpurs cinched just below the knee, and a Harris-tweed jacket over a blindingly white shirt with a jaunty open collar, leaps gracefully over the low door and lands, breaking his ankle.

"We'll call in your understudy for the next round–ha, ha!" cries M from the top of the steps, moving aside to let a fleet of valets, all decked out as nurses, pass by.

The procession enters a grand hall dominated by an enormous stained–glass window, and puts the stretcher down on a divan poised between two potted palms in blue Chinese faience.

Coming apart at the seams! You're just trying to make the rest of us feel better, aren't you? Well, take a look at this revealing a vicious blue scar beneath his shirt *always reminds me of Normandy-Niemen* giving an affectionate elbow in the ribs to the unknown guest grey face + bulging eyes. *Let's have a look at this,* ripping open the trouser-leg, *now don't scream like that – it's not all that bad. We'll find you some decent camouflage for dinner.*

Into the dressing–room, find slacks and matching jacket more or less the size of the wounded, who, at a glance, I'd say is 42–16–22.

I profit from the occasion to remind the new assistant (his first day on the job) of certain principles to be maintained no matter what the circumstance, such as # 1: Unity and Economy: "The means must concur with the communally desired ends." Which doesn't mean you should ruin the dish for fear of adding a little spice, no, no, no, absolutely not, but you must bow to superior taste with a deft sleight of hand (a case tailor-made for the phrase), rising above contradiction and avoiding the marriage of goldfish and rabbit, of which we suffer entirely too much these days. # 2: Sacrifice: "Learn to repress strokes of pure aesthetic genius in favor of greater efficiency." Avoid outrageous hyper-realism, such as the reconstruction of a brain in cauliflower to serve alongside braised cervelle, or turbulent seas of sculpted spinach surrounding the fish and other such idiocies, I insist in parentheses, raising my voice slightly to engrave it into his memory. # 3: Serenity: "When in doubt, show restraint."

He gives me a blank stare – pale, empty

eyes – mouth hanging open, ready to swallow a passing fly. I give up. Give me that one–the yellow one.

The yellow one – quick!

You're limp as a dead fish, my boy. Get it into gear – this isn't a convalescent home.

In fact, that's the one thing that it positively is not. Do yourself a favor and get that straight right now if you want the privileges – such as being left in peace – that the others already enjoy thanks to their loyal and diligent service.

I've chosen something casual in a pale yellow pin–stripe that looks like it should suit the occasion. On the other hand, I could go for this light grey one, just let out the hem a little, but, no, no, that's a delicate operation, what with the crease and all – and no more time to dither about, ring of the bell *drrrring* urgent.

These days, you've got to change your attitude – work not only more but *better*. It's the work itself that's changed. No more *Yesssir, got a job* and hop! into a hammock for the rest of your life.

Take this new guy – he's either got early Alzheimer's or a tsetse virus; he's looking at me like an anvil just fell on his head.

Total service – think way beyond the task at hand, I continue.

Which is to say don't stand around waiting for a thank you – get it?

Nor applause.

Get this suit downstairs on the double dring–dring hurry up, tuck in those elbows, let's go, chop–chop dring–dring chop–chop.

2

All right then. Just relax until dinner. First gong, in the salon. Second gong, at the table. Not too complex, I hope? You'll find a smoking jacket in your room, said M to the unknown guest stretched out effigy–style on a camp bed in the hall.

— *What are you mumbling about? What? the others? Yes, yes, they've all arrived. Everybody's in his room. By bus, yes, yesterday evening. What? All right, by "coach" if you prefer, but let's not get all worked up over semantics, eh? We'll say motorized carriage – will that please you? Is Mr. Whatzit here? No – no Whatzit. Whatzit missed the call. His wife too – you like her, eh? Those brunettes – hot stuff.*

— Confused / shameful / ridiculous / sorry / the lips of the injured let a few shards of tortured phrasing escape. *My / my / leg / trou / trousers too tight / fu / idiot / 2 m 03 Fosbury style /long time ago / sorry about the trouble / broken?*

— *No, no – if it was broken, you'd really be in pain. This is nothing. Let me have a look at it, pal.*

Yeah, the foot's pretty bad – looks painful. How's that feel there?

Scream.

– Yeah, I'll bet. It's up to you of course, but I'd say operate right away – otherwise, gangrene. And that goes into overdrive in no time – you'll be black as a Zulu before you can count to three. But if we amputate right now, we can save you. Here, take a swig of this upending a flask of cognac into his mouth with one hand, grabbing a saw with the other. *It'll be – how can I put it – a difficult moment, but afterwards "Resurrection." Otherwise, maggots.* Blood spurted onto the carpet, and our guest was already showing the whites of his eyes as M finished with the saw and his assistant poured the rest of the cognac over the stump as a disinfectant.

The Db4 stops on a dime. The unknown guest opens the door and alights with dignity and grace.

Folds up his shades and slips them, in one smooth move, into the upper left pocket of his anthracite flannel blazer. Before replying to my respectful salutations with a dull half–

cough, he cocks his finger toward the luggage in the trunk, pivots neatly on his heel and turns his back on me to admire the view. Light late–afternoon mist. 18:45. Dinner will be served in 105 minutes.

And then, nothing happens. Suspended calm for several minutes. It'll be all right, breathing normal, nothing unusual has occurred. He has not broken his ankle.

There are no tire tracks in the gravel.

All is well.

Both arms hang at rest, hands relaxed, breathe. Breathe, stretch, breathe. Flex. Eyes on the horizon, exhale. Calm.

3

Bring me a drink! wakes me up with a start. Quick transition to the vertical, open hidden service door. Must wake up instantly. But not too thoroughly or it slows you down.

Ultrarapid descent of emergency spiral staircase, arriving at office in 23.1 seconds. I'm out of shape.

Just not up to speed.

One solid pound of very dry ice cubes into shaker, splash of vermouth. Strain once, triple measure of gin + extra dash, strain again. The cooks are giving me really weird looks. Pour. Place glass on tray, activate lift, which opens automatically as soon as it reaches the moving panel in the library. Enter room, head clear, thinking nothing, looking straight toward the enormous snowflakes besieging the Assyrian windows of the corner salon.

Half-turn to the right, straight ahead. Stop, present tray.

— *Hitler used to say we're a country of hicks who just could end up leading the fashion industry*, M is saying, speaking to the ceiling, his head tilted back and resting on the ornate cushions of the couch, *and you know he's not wrong, though a few things have changed. But not all that much, eh?* with a generalized glance over the guests.

— *We'd all be collective-farm whores or (...) gentlemen-farmer-collectors?* M continues, eyes on the ceiling, *or breeders, if you think of the mating business for the Whatever Derby as a rural pastime or of collecting Boulle consoles as limited to a stylistic caprice.*

— *Boulle consoles go for up to 10 million pounds*, interjects a little man with an elongated cranium, a Pickwick Club suit, a bow tie, and steel-rimmed glasses.

— *Dzing-boum-bom tagada*, cries the unknown guest, suddenly zipping across the room doing a goosestep.

Polite laughter and resumption of conversation in small groups.

— *He's not wrong*, comments the unknown guest, perched on a library ladder, *today we call*

it the CIZ—the Cottage Industry Zone—the boys are in
their element, wood-workers, marionette makers, all
sorts of small enterprises. And believe me, they "mix"
well, though I won't draw you a picture, ooooh no.
All bearded and not just sucking ice cubes, I promise
you (…)

— *We know* interrupts a white-haired woman dryly *we saw it all in the nudist exposé.*

— *They do their shopping stark naked in monk's sandals. At the butcher's, it's matching colors,* insists Pickwick with the glasses.

— *That's exactly what I mean,* throws in the unknown guest in a single breath. *It's precisely that. That's just how I see it. I see it just like you do (…). It's great to think that you share your neighbors' opinions; you say to yourself, I'm not wrong after all, it's an extraordinary sensation and – how can I put it – personally, I think that we've got to uh (…)*

— *Ahhhhhh,* interjects M in a pseudo-yawn to cut short the effusion.

I'm still standing mid-salon. Listening slows you down. Control hold, finger on tray. Cross the red carpet.

Crepe soles good grip maximum adherence. March straight, dignified gaze fixed along an imaginary line that runs from a point on the wall behind me to the central windows ahead, already obscured by snow.

How can it coat the facade so evenly, given all its minute protrusions, if the placement of each flake is unpredictable (wind, etc.)? *And you'll be serving that glass any year now, I suppose?* interrupts my thoughts just as I'm about to hit on a perfectly luminous explanation *what the hell are you doing just standing there?* screams M.

4

I cross the yards and yards of red Persian carpet that separate us.

Quick glance at picture in book open on table.

Profound absorption – click. Box: 30 by 15 by 7 deep containing a miniature garden surrounding a pond, framed by the sides of the box, which form the walls. The leaves of the trees, done in an oxidized bronze, are too large for the trunks.

Sycamores, says the caption. 11th dynasty.

Scale model? For what? Whose dynasty? And the microscopic birds that must be hidden among those enormous leaves, what are they like?

If I could, I'd be right in there with them. Doing well. I'm there and I'm staying. It's the life I've always dreamed of. I curl around the branches like an acrobat on his trapeze.

It's all as it should be.

I'm on the other side, within the pocket of

air carved out of the void hidden behind the green. In nature's holding pattern, suspended, left out of the census. I've got regular feathers; in a minute, I'll be whistling "Ooh ooh, I'm Rob," Oh no...I'm going to whistle...don't...don't...oh no...I'm whistling – *What the hell are you doing with your mouth all puckered up like a chicken's ass?*

– *WHAT ARE YOU DOING? Has milord taken an interest in Egyptian art?* Glance around the circled guests + eyes on the ceiling. *Which isn't an art, properly speaking, as it is, above all, funerary, which is to say, practical,* he just can't help digressing for the edification of all present. *Here, here, take the book, yes, yes, take it – and later, they'll be talking to me about "cultural exchange."*

I continue to hold the tray out to him, subtly dropping my gaze and complementing it with the slightest suggestion of a modest smile = no, no, milord knows quite well that never, but never, etc. He grabs the glass and downs it in a single gulp.

–*The class struggle,* he continues, hopping up onto a little stage erected for eventual musicians.

The class struggle
it's just lip-service we all know
it's every man for himself

All right then, so it does no good
to try and help a guy

There comes a time they've got to grow up
you hand 'em everything on a silver platter
and all for nothing

–Fine, thanks, go, that's all, he says to me, as I bend over to sweep up an infinitesimal cigar ash from the floor, now on all fours on the carpet. I'm so far down here on the ground, I can barely hear his voice. It's insane, he says.

It's the same with politics
tell folks don't do that
and they do it

Seeing as they're going to do it anyway
tell them to do the opposite, etc.

– It's like watching the goalie, the unknown guest interjects. *If I think he's going to go for the right, he goes for the left, but if he knows that I know that he's planning to go to the left, he'll go to the left, and turn it inside out.*

– That's what my cousin always told me, M goes on, ignoring the interruption. *He's an absolute moron, but he has his visionary moments. They're so rare he never notices them himself, which is, in its own way, a mark of genius. He always says predictions are useless. For example, he says: There are no corners in the market where you can stash money away ad vitam.*

So no one does anything
and–zip–the idea's been stolen.

It's just like in the pogroms
tell the guys to take off split get out of here

They stay
no doubt held back by purely material
considerations.

–You wonder how some people can hesitate be-
tween life and a pair of matching chairs, he continues, sitting down gruffly tired. *Though for these*
that you treat like plastic– I'd think twice.

I'm stretched out across the pattern of the
central carpet, which involves an intricate red
and green labyrinth. If you plaster your eye
right up against it, you can follow it. A my-
opic promenade at the level of dust.

I'm a crumb in the hedges of green wool,
my name is thing, Mr. Whatzit, Rob, I know
not, I'm swallowed up in the paths of paradise, I sing with closed mouth "Curious / It's
not a rose I touch / It's always you." I hear
nothing more. I'm a crumb in the hedges of
green wool, my name is thing. Turn left. I'm a
crumb in the hedges of green wool, my name
is thing. Turn right. I'm a crumb in the
hedges of green wool; my name is thing.

I really wonder what good it is and for whom
this democracy of feelings

me, I think this
and me, I think that

It's nuts this notion
that the common people should have their say
where does that come from?

—We know it only too well, replies the unknown guest.

It's a new idea
there's "soul everywhere"
you might as well let the ducks and chickens vote
what are you doing still here?

What the hell are you doing? Very slowly I realize that this question is being addressed to me. Already far away, lost in the paths of red and green fibers, having almost reached the center of paradise without having once gone over the line, hopping on one foot.

I'm a crumb in the hedges of green wool; my name is thing. I'm a crumb in the hedges of green wool; my name is thing. Blind among all these fronds, I sweep up the microscopic ash and leave.

5

I slip on my mid–weight outdoor uniform – not forgetting to buckle on the gadget–filled leather holster under my shirt. Camo trousers in oilcloth. Non–skid boots with reinforced steel toes. Multi–pocket vest containing precision screwdriver, multi–blade knife, spoon + folding fork, ultraflat flask of denatured alcohol, needles, sutures, and scalpel with changeable blades. Hatwise, I choose the #5 Davy–Crockett summer model in light lynx equipped with an air–filtration mask that folds out from under the ear–flaps. Automatic in case of noxious fogs or blinding and/or aggressive smoke.

Bamboo fishing pole, $8\frac{1}{2}$ foot rapid action, fingerless driving gloves, anti–UV glasses with a micro–sensor hidden in the frame that picks up every sound down to the slightest footstep of an ant climbing a blade of grass.

After hours of running across fields, leaping old stone fences and nettle-filled trenches, I'm feeling calm. No one ever comes here. At least, not for the same reason I do. I'm here and I'm staying.

I run I sing "O my oh so lovely Valentine oof oof / oof oof, I run in the woods of blue cedar / the twigs snap under the iron of my boots / My name is John Robinson / I am the field runner / My name is John Robinson, son of Rob / I come down the mountains / The son of the red-breasted robin / Oof oof.

I'm at the edge of a precipice overhanging a waterfall at the end of a green gorge.

A little dam produces a cascade that oxygenates the water and at the same time attracts a group of fish that align themselves beneath it like bombers in the sky.

I prepare a five foot long, rapid-action rod equipped with a 34 pound line ending in a #8 or 10 hook onto which I fix a grasshopper preceded by an English soft-lead weight. I slink silently across the field, nose in the grass, then whip my arm back and then forward, sending the line projecting over the water hole in an arc, snap.

My shadow looms dangerously over the water, so I decide to become smaller as only I know how to do.

The landscape becomes larger, except for certain nearby objects, which stay my scale so it doesn't get too nightmarish.

The fine, transparent layer that slides like glass over the stones becomes thicker. Sounds grow.

Rolling of pebbles + sound of foam.

Everything shifts – the grasses become trees, the banks, cliffs, the verges, forests. I walk barefoot through irises as tall as a man, I run. I sing "In the hot / scent of the fields / La–la, la–la." Shoulders swallowed up in the giant grass. Lost meat through the towering thistles. Robinson – that's me.

I jerk lightly on the line to give the dead grasshopper a lively look across the surface of the pond. Raising the oxygen level, the cascade activates the particles floating on the water. Little drifting fetuses suspended in the cold; perfect corpses for the squadron in ambush.

Fish just love this surprise plankton.

Me too.

I give the string a few more jerks. The whole time the grasshopper's been sitting there, it's been looking just like what it is: a plain old decapitated grasshopper with a head of green wool. The dam makes a sound like a gas cylinder with a permanent leak, its minute changes in pressure just like a chainsaw slowing down deep in the woods.

Everything's just like everything else.

It's marvelous.

The rot that collects in the corners of all half-living things has the sweet taste of the film that's just like the gangrene on an arm that is in turn like the packed dirt under a plank and the gas of decomposition threading into the cold night.

That's how I see it. It's extraordinary.

Everything is in everything.

It's marvelous.

I fix the light froth that still persists in the

darkness with the question in my mind occu-
pying more and more of the space available
for thought. The still–persistent in the dark
lightness of the froth. The in–the–dark persistent lightness of the froth. Question.

The more–and–more pressing question.

The question: What happens to fish in the
dark? I fall asleep in the grass.

6

With infinite precaution, I follow the curve of the lacquered wall along the grand corridor as I carry the platter. 30 yards, murmur of voices growing as I approach the dining room. 20 yards, slight inclination of platter to compensate for curve. 10 yards, murmur, I get closer.

Curve 60 degrees in front of the consoles, click tongue, open door by pushing simultaneously on the two hidden latches. I enter, lights up, exclamations.

–*It's so beeauuuutiful ahhhhhh!* a trio at the end of the table cries, *so beautiful. What a fish!*

–*From around here? Right out front?* asks the unknown guest in a shrill voice, *from that ditch? From those black pools?*

–*From the lake!* screeches a wiry, jumpy guy. *Bang, battle!*

–*In the days when there were carp in what you call our "black pools"* says M, *and you couldn't have said it better since the dam dates from the Hundred Years War and from the Prince of the same color, well, in our "black pools" as you call them, which certain of the informed call Moats, there were enormous carp, and they were eaten stuffed, and not stuffed with just anything, I'll have you know, but with moray eels.*

The white-haired woman with the black three-cornered hat applauds and gestures wildly in a 'thumbs-down' move.

Laughter.

I sweep my eyes around 180 degrees, squinting in order to memorize the blurred faces of the guests, comparing the shadows with the names memorized from the seating plan.

I turn and set the platter on the sideboard. Two brief breaths. Twitch the nose out of superstition. *I'm going to make bad memories go away.* Kick-turn, approach table.

Platter direction left toward female guest #1, pause 2 inches from her fingers with a gentle swing that coordinates the arm and the shoulder, placing the body's weight forward. Finish off the gesture with an invisible shift of the wrist, suggest that she serve her–self from the pike, presented in a curve to represent the bend in the river where the fish was caught, munching a shrimp, on a bed of semolina to suggest sand, click.

I could not possibly drop the platter; I will not drop the platter, these are my two hands holding the platter – no possible problem. I've been in service since time began.

I nod my head toward my assistant like a pianist cuing his page–turner: *Start the sauce*. Adds a human dimension to the choreography.

Take two steps back, freeze. Relax.

– *I've heard that there's a monster in your moat,* snickers the unknown guest.

– *Ridiculous, utterly ridiculous it's an hal...*, smothered sounds from M who goes on, *hallu... hallucination*, tapping quickly against his forehead with his red napkin, quite happy to launch into an adored theme: *People always get these fixed ideas, absurd beliefs.*

People get these fixed ideas
absurd beliefs

Pegasus and the unicorn
are downright scientific by comparison
hard and pure

Mere servants' notions
"me me I got an idea M'ster!"
god help us

– *There are those who say there's a monster in your moat*, pursues the unknown guest, *unbelievable!*, to give the impression that he'd said it ironically the first time. Incredible! he continues with a hyena–like snicker and spasmodic jerks of his chin, trying to elicit a *Yes-of-course* from the table in general. Last attempt at being droll.

I can't listen to everything, I have work to do. I pay attention to my work. I slide my arm forward, make a supple half–swivel, the body's weight hovering over the table. I serve, I pay attention. *I destroy bad memories.* I hum in order to forget that there's something I must forget, my striated crepe soles grip the gleaming parquet.

I'm experienced. I've got a will of iron. I'm simply impeccable. I will not drop the platter.

Smooth, frictionless labor.

I articulate each action as I perform it.

I'm in perfect control.

I'm there, that's me, those are my hands holding the platter, there's no problem, I see the platter, and very softly I hum the song that keeps me and my actions in real time.

I am I and no one else.

I will not drop the platter. Three more people to serve, no one hears my song. I sing very softly between my teeth, I smile ever so slightly, I'm a machine incapable of error, I'm supple and coordinated, I'm a perfect object.

– *What absolutely unbelievably grotesque idiots – it's the last straw!* screams M his eyes bulging, mouth gaping open. *Absolutely the last straw!*

Does he practice that in front of the mirror?

Riveted by shock like a rabbit before a fox

that's suddenly the size of a bear *and they want us to believe in democracy. Well all right, good luck with these guys who have an opinion on everything, he continues. We'll end up holding a referendum on what to have for breakfast. But do take something nonetheless – you'll fade away to nothing if you carry on like that,* he snaps at Guest #8, a depressive type with huge teeth and shoulders shrunken à l'anglaise who, dazed by tranquilizers, is forgetting to serve herself while she sits mesmerized by the dismemberment of a huge leg of lamb running with grease. *Who pays, huh?* he screams.

Who pays in the end
who pays the subsidies?

They'll be in our place soon
it amounts to the same thing
there's always a high and a low

I leave, trusting the rest of the service to my assistants. The really big things have all been accomplished.

All went admirably.

All is well. Calm. Relax. It's done. Pure workmanship. 100% success.

With the exception of that disagreeable moment when M said to the person at the end of the table to (maybe?) keep him from making a blunder: *Stop, he could understand.*

– He-he-he is [ ] he has [ ] he showed a-a-a [ ] his [ ], stuttered the red-head in the apple-green leg-of-mutton sleeves, pointing at me. Though I'd been doing nothing unusual.

– *Stop, he could understand,* cut off M, effectively saying by this gesture that #1 I was something better left unsaid and that I had acted "badly." And that #2 I do not know this language code. And that #3 I will continue to become more and more that which is better left unsaid forever.

The *Stop* sounded like a Shhh! and all I heard of the rest was something like "Coudanderstam." A Dutch chivalric hero? An incantation to suppress the evil eye? *Shhh Coudanderstam!* A line from A Mid-summer's Night's Dream? Ciel mon mari!? Listen, someone's coming! Not so loud, someone could hear us!?!

I know perfectly well how to camouflage the voice–duck sounds, for instance–as the situation requires.

7

One two breathe deep ok off you go straight–
en right leg out with a snap. Swing it forward.
Plant the foot. Flex the knees. That's it.

Second stride left leg. Raise it gra–d–u–a–
ll–y sixth stride. Carbon stored up from nour–
ishment combines with nitrogen in the mus–
cles. Head tilted slightly forward. 10 s 45/100.

Not great.

Accelerate by rowing with your arms,
pushing as much air behind you as possible.
Hands held slightly cupped. Don't let up for
at least 60 yards. I keep my blood sugar on
hold until my foot hits the track. Facial mus–
cles beat along mechanically, keeping time.

On we go.

Descend into valley leaping fences. Inte–
grated greens of the tunnel beneath the over–
hanging trees. 3 mile. Don't slow down. Head
back and feet pounding on. Yes! Entirely
aerodynamically hip profile crossing verdant
landscape. 4 mile.

Got to get in shape.

Just not up to my usual form. Low blood sugar. Something's wrong. There's no use denying it.

Low blood sugar.

Nitrogen in muscles not good.

Carbon reserve zero.

I vary the absorption according to the information furnished by my acceleration sensors.

I shift into second wind – yes! Sudden influx of air into muscle fiber snaps those weakened zones right into shape.

Dr. Good–morning. Dr. Be-Good-to-yourself-this-morning. Dr. Be-good–to-yourself. 14 miles.

I constrict the angle of my clavicle simultaneously with that of my left nostril. Unleashing great strides. I'm running beautifully.

But I'm just not quite as fast. 15 miles.

I've slowed down. There's no denying it. The beta–blockers are no longer doing their job between the organs.

The poisons in the air are heading straight for my deepest tissues.

The little evil particles carried by the air swarm in spirals like bees honing in on their target. These tiny particles are composed of insect bacteria + fish viruses + infected pollen + etc.

The air is full of animals.

8

Ten o'clock, milord, I say in a clear, ringing voice as I walk over to the window. Tray in hand, mail sorted, newspaper ironed.

Pull the cord that opens the enormous curtain to reveal the still-sleeping country-side that looks just like a painting by ?

That "artist" who seems to have camped here forever – what's his name? Turn? Turned? Turnip? He's like a fish in water. Eats at the big table. Sleek, starched, stuffed. Until he has to show some results.

So, what have you painted here?

Not much if you think of the 3/4 of every day he's spent stretched out on a park bench clearly not studying the contours of a cumulus.

As one who intends to be a painter should.

– *Paintings.*

What paintings? Those scribbles on scraps of blue paper from the deli? With the money he's saving, you'd think he could buy some normal white paper.

Scenes all blurred. Start by learning how to draw people. Or maybe just wear glasses.

Or maybe you have a problem (*I can't paint*) in which case, admit it.

Admit it, it's blurry. How can you miss it! It's incredible.

And everyone swoons and goes *Oh yes, yes, your work is so-o-o-o interesting.*

I'm going to serve him up a list of every–thing he's eaten.

On such–and–such a day: a leg of lamb

On such–and–such a day: a rabbit, etc.

I'm going to tell him: that's what it all adds up to. And I'm not even counting the linens or all the trouble you've caused. Just what you've eaten since the day you arrived.

You got to get him to pitch in a little like the others always do, milord, I add aloud.

If milord will permit me to say so.

Shut up! the still–sleeping head replies, holding out its hand for the dressing gown with the Brandenburg monogram *not in the morning, never in the morning.*

Instantly unfold tray table. Remove metal dome from plate. Omelet à la menthe, #3 sausage, smoked breast, braised tomatoes, green beans in juice of mutton, toast.

Open paper.

There must be a way to avoid the use of the third person, which slows you down. If it would please milord, etc.

Use a different approach. Don't say: If milord would like to take a look at page 4, where there's a picture of the scene of the crime that so intrigues milord. Say: look at on which it's of the scene of the that so intrigues crime <u>Page 4.</u>

The important word at the end; that way people listen to you and don't cut you off.

And here's the boiled but not too long served on toast lightly spread with parsley butter Eggs.

Breakfast is served.

9

I glance over his shoulder to get my own good look at page 4. Plain little house very dark due to cheap printing.

Photo of family all lined up. Certain heads circled in white to identify the victims. Followed by a series of enlargements of dark lumps in the grass indicating places where the earth had recently been disturbed along the base of a row of elms like you see bordering lots of people's properties.

How very strange. If I'd murdered them, I wouldn't have buried them outside my own front door. *Man Buries Own Family Under Front Lawn.* Huge headline four columns wide.

They're going to hold another inquest.

The inspector must be saying to himself that the one person who absolutely could not be guilty is the man who lives just in front of the place they found the bodies. Ideal alibi. No reasonable criminal is going to bury his victims in his own garden.

There's something fishy here milord, I say a bit too loudly.

– *Give me a break, would you? Not in the morning. How many times do I have to tell you: Not in the morning. Which word don't you understand?*

Would milord like me to trim his moustache?

– *Tomorrow.*

Close eyes retrace path to own room. File images of burial mounds in memory folder. Label it Crime in order not to lose it.

It's mine.

Slide at will into the black and white grains of the elms. Open up the aperture for contrast. Part the weave of branches. Pass beyond into the void within.

Slip inside the cage of air formed by the network of branches.

Wait for the birds. Wait for someone to come looking for you. I'm like them; I'm all right. I've got the Robinson Syndrome. Chest out, head up, breath light, and whistling.

All is well. They'll never find me.

As I move forward, the little sounds get

louder, voices from various floors, footsteps overhead, doors creaking, distant whispers.

Wait for evening because the darkness muffles noise. The sounds of daytime drain into the holes in the ground that let the earth breathe. The sounds that remain of half–living things that have disappeared when you hear nothing more. I go back to them.

Then wait to hear that there is no more sound. The time it takes for each sound at the bottom of each thing to stop. The time it takes each thing to stop the time to get back to them.

10

Late morning. I go out and I listen.

I hide under an overturned shell in the pond, breathing through a bamboo pipe, then begin my approach.

I close in on my target in graceful spirals. Belly to the ground, I toss stones in the opposite direction – it's a decoy to distract the people lounging in deck chairs a little apart from the main group. More aware of surrounding sounds, they raise their heads and look, but see nothing back there where I am not.

This is how I move in on them.

But underwater it's impossible.

Not because of the breathing problem, and not because a bamboo shoot traveling along all by itself in the middle of a pond is a dead-give-away, but because the shallow waters demand that one remain absolutely still in order to avoid suspicious ripples.

And absolutely still is impossible.

Hiding in a haystack is another option, the advantage being mobility – you can change location, fine-tune the reception as it were by simply hopping the haystack along. This has its dangers, however, such as finding yourself upside-down in a ditch, tripping over a root, etc. You can also simply build a network of underground tunnels, with spy-holes positioned where the people in question are statistically most likely to gather. But such people have a nasty habit of changing their minds *why don't we go sit over there for once? Oh yes, that would be fun!* A thrill a minute.

Actually, the listening is best up in the trees.

Out there on the end of a branch, it's like being right at the tip of an antenna. The perfect post for deciphering voices rising up between the leaves.

The warmth of the sunlight filtered and scattered by the interlocking leaves is hypnotic. I could fall asleep up here. The play of light filtered through leaves is the perfect camouflage. Zebra-striping or zouave-bird.

The alternating bands of warm and cool on my cheek are putting me to sleep.

I'm about to fall asleep.

I'm going to fall asleep and fall out of the tree.

If you observe a beehive very carefully — if you're a fan of the habitat as I am, chirps the unknown guest, *you see of course that the Queen Mother Bee gets screwed by the same male several times, which means that in addition to having a whole slew of half-sisters, they have a certain number of super-sisters in common. With whom they share rich chromosomal affinities .*

Fascinating, says a man whose face I can't see as it's hidden by the branches.

The greater or lesser speed of the beating wings indicates the distance, and the position of the body, and the direction of the targeted flower.

Fascinating.

All-righty then, interjects a woman with gold teeth, *you're looking great, love. Go see how lunch is coming along and then hurry back here and finish the guided tour.*

Creak of lawn-chair as the guy gets up,

followed at a respectable distance by "He's a changed man," and "I told you not to invite him."

As far as bees are concerned, it's always a beautiful day because their sense of color — so different from our own — is virtually nil. Blue and yellow at best, adds the guy — re-creaking of lawn-chair– having come right back, top speed. But when it comes to flowers, that's another story.

Hand 'em an unknown flower
and they don't need a bunch of laboratory testing
to know that it's worth their while

They're not like us
they know how to learn
from the experience of others

You should write something on that, says the woman with the gold teeth after a very long silence, the public would be just wild about it. The vinegar murmur of her voice wakes me up like a shot in the head.

Oh wouldn't I look just splendid sliding out of the tree asleep. Like a rotten apple or a squirrel dying of a heart attack landing on your head. I'm right above Gold–Tooth who's on a tape loop *write something on that write write.*

Body wound around the branches; livery, green.

Spy cap, no one's going to spot me.

It's great.

11

They move. Keep following.

Where are they going?

Come down the tree like a fireman down a pole. I hide in the rhododendrons, choosing the ones that match my outfit.

I can't quite catch everything they say *this world of ours today there's something how can I put it*, muses M, as he takes a turn around a clump of buttercup-yellow zinnias, *horrible don't you think* tapping his cane on the gravel in time to "We'll Get Them Yet" *the planet Mars! the planet Mars!* with a continuous background drone of affirmation on the part of the unknown guest, making one last-ditch effort.

Third turn around the zinnias. *People will say anything. It's too much.*

We need a governmental decree to extract
a priori this mental gangrene

If a citizen has a rotten limb
cut it off no time to stand around and talk about it

And if there's no more ether Major
you go ahead with it anyway

Bite down on that my boy
stick a bit between his teeth
and off you go.

"*Absolutely,*" says the unknown guest, at‑tempting congeniality in spite of it all, *it's like yesterday, I heard a local say that there really is a monster in that lake and that he had pictures — said he'd show them to me anytime — said his brother-in-law, the mechanic, had taken them himself on the spot of the Miracle, etc.*

"They're morons," insists Pickwick.

"*Same thing,*" continues the unfortunate guest, "*same thing with the "The Crime Next Door." You saw the pictures this morning. Hyped-up gossip to stir up the folks who go for the sensational. Those mounds of earth, that's bullshit, a monstrous inven‑tion. Why on earth would a guy who'd killed his whole family in a fit of brain fever go and bury them in front of his own door? "But tell me, Inspector,"* adopting the voice of an aging lunatic, *"if I'm really the one who did it, why would I have gone and buried them in front of my own door with my name engraved on a plaque above the doorbell?"* But the cop's not falling for it, etc. And bing!

Yep, that's it, you got it, M replies, not even hearing him out then screaming in the deaf cousin's ear *we've got to do something*.

We've got to do something.
I'm not talking about bringing in the army
no need to go that far
just a little turn of the screw, eh?

Yes, yes, yes, yes, yes, yes, yes, M keeps time at the head of the little procession.

The flowerbed around which the speakers are turning, followed by family and allies in small groups arranged according to their var–ied emotions, is a mound of earth planted with yellow zinnias, above which rises a Group of Playing Children circled by a path that's already less visible than it was the first time around.

Yes, yes, yes, yes, yes, yes, yes, inaudible comments chopped into pieces with each clipped turn because night has fallen and the melted dark lump that is the group-to-be-spied-upon swallows up the sounds of the words.

It's the darkness that swallows up the words.

Hidden in a blind spot trying to overhear. Invisible shoes. Trousers blending into evening. Disappeared. I'm way at the back of the darkness. Hanging out with a big-headed insect, a lumpy little toad, a branch of an old pear tree, and weeds.

12

No, that's not it at all, I tell them, after a rather long silence. Employee lounge, long table, rustic scenes inlaid in paneling.

The old traditions of our profession – they're over, done, gone, I tell them, getting up to write on the board:

$$\left(\frac{B}{P}\right)^n$$

B, that's "Before." P, that's "Progress." The new pace will reduce time requirements by a thousand percent.

Get it: your old ways (even if they look the same to everyone else, even if they all say "it's just like before") must be raised exponentially by new and imperceptible actions.

"'Imperceptible,' I don't get it," says the butcher's assistant.

It's like those images of the devil that superimpose themselves on a gorgeous sunset,

I explain as calmly as possible. You're not really sure you've seen them, but they leave a bad feeling in the air.

My affectionate tone reassures them.

They leave a bad feeling. A very, very bad feeling. I scream more or less right in his face.

He sniffles and lowers his eyes.

That one, I'm going to have to train him from the ground up.

Gentlemen, I continue, service has changed. The very concept has changed. I relax my facial muscles, crinkle up my eyes and raise them to the ceiling.

The very concept. Why?

Dead silence.

Because conditions have changed. I rise and begin pontificating: No longer used to being served in the great tradition which has made our country's reputation, the gentry has forgotten. Moral: we've got to add in little extras to let them know that the work is being done to perfection.

"In every way we've got to pay more attention because they've forgotten," cries the chauffeur. *"It's*

like a car that's been sitting in the garage for thirty years."

That's it, I scream.

I'm going to raise that guy right up to the top, he's my right-hand man, there's hope, there's help, things are moving forward.

If you serve lapin à la royale, you have to put a little crown on its head just to let them know what it is.

"*A crown of what?*" asks the butcher's assistant.

It makes you wonder.

You have to underline each gesture, exaggerate a little, show them how it's done. I forge on. You've got to dissect every movement. Demonstrate the sleight of hand and fancy footwork involved at every stage.

Today's topic: "Crumbing."

Two techniques?

— *The scraper and the the the?* stutters the butcher's assistant, *the little thing you roll across the table that has the little crumb-catcher underneath.*

The crumber! I scream. Take thumb/index, control with ring-finger, arm-wrist-hand become a single unit, that's the secret. Always pull toward the crumb, from in front to behind, never push the crumb. Risk of sending it flying – giving it a running jump, as it were, etc. Add a subtle shift of the hips, small, discrete, just enough to give a bit of rhythm to the act, like that, see?

To add a little style, no?

– *Yes*, says the butcher's assistant.

NO I scream, to drive the crumber toward the objective while preventing it from skating all over the table, even into spots where there are no crumbs. Gains time and creates subconscious sense of security in the diner, total service, admiration that reflects upon our master, and therefore upon us.

– *And therefore upon us*, repeats the group, riveted.

Good, I scream, good–good–good. Conclusion: we must know everything about the client, down to the last button. Tendencies, desires, potential for modification of tastes. The curve of needs and satisfactions.

And naturally, that's only the tip of the

iceberg. With that I've gone too far–I rise and throw myself against the blackboard, furiously drawing circles and ovals like they do to illustrate set theory, screaming all the while: The asymptote of a line of improved work never truly and rightly reaches perfection, but comes infinitely closer and closer.

Cough. Sit back down. And into the abounding silence, I list the subjects to be covered next time. Pause. Then slowly raise my eyes and drop a condescending "You are dismissed."

13

The well–diffused light reveals the river bottom, no weeds, yellow stones. The ripples on the surface herd the insects toward a single point where, as if caught in a natural net, the dreamed–of fish is lying: 2 pounds, black speckled scales, pink gills, tapered body, quick eye.

The heat simmers classically over the fields. Like the rippled fumes of gasoline look like water wrinkling the landscape or strangling a tree. Like when you look at a chair with your eyes full of tears. Like a stick standing in water that seems to fold itself in two. Like the jet stream behind a plane dissolving into clouds.

That's how I see it. It's marvelous.

I haven't moved for so long that I've become like a reed, a huge blade of grass, a log in the shadows *the people I love are mixed up in terrible things* two electric blue dragonflies perch on my ears. All's well.

The coveted fish is there.

Without moving a muscle, I slowly extend my hand to release the catch on the reel, then give the ultra-light pole just the right flick, unleashing a full five yards of line in an arc above my head to position the Ryman III dry fly with steel highlights absolutely perfectly. Four times, each one just as perfect. But the fish doesn't budge, too busy watching his little slice of river go by.

Just what I ought to be doing if I ever truly want to understand his motives.

So I cover my body with plaster, let it dry, and then remove the shell in two careful halves. Then melt some tires. Pour a layer of melted rubber into each half. Join the two halves with adjustable leather straps. Insert a clear plastic window at eye-level. Paint the whole thing the color of water.

Attach little balls of lead at the waist and a flexible rubber tube (say a radiator hose) at the mouth. Then slip silently into the current. Anchor myself to the riverbed with a metal stake, stay motionless and watch the river from inside while the fish get used to my presence.

Gaze forever at all the little things upstream caught in the transparent block. Study the particular speed of things underwater. They appear quicker from above and slower from below.

Hide the whole thing, after oiling it to protect it, in waterproof wooden box buried near the spot in order to avoid the risk inherent in crossing the lawn in a diving outfit. Which would require me (as a supposed stranger) to say hello.

Ravens.

Ravens.

I don't move a muscle. They keep swooping down and casting disrupting shadows on the riverbed. Retreat underground or make a diversion?

Best solution: post a natural-looking fox and owl in little hiding places, equipped with a simple "pop-up" device operated by a pedal. Pedal retracts cover, up comes head of fox. Intense and protracted response from ravens:

caw, caw, caw, etc.

Repeat the experiment five times; each time, less reaction.

Switch places with the fox: reaction medium.

Do this three times, soon no reaction at all, the birds are used to it, but still ready to fly off screeching at the slightest hint of new danger. Bring on owl; start again.

Pretty soon nothing could frighten those birds.

Repeat routine with scarecrow that looks more or less like me. Stringy, colorless hair draped over carved pumpkin stuck on top of sack of potatoes.

They'll never get used to me.

Goodbye.

14

Return to house. My room. Large painting in black frame: Francis Remington, Two figures, Indians. On the right, a watercolor: Max Thorpe, Duck. Dead.

The functional furniture is all arranged along the walls. Butcher-block table, card table, clock-stand, file cabinets, recording console with frosted glass partitions, table with enlarger, folding bookcase-bed, retro-projector, display-cases, soldering post.

Need life-sized mannequins for practicing ventriloquism; can't find time to get them – first time I've ever gotten behind in my program.

I'm slowing down. That's all there is to it.

I'm just not in shape. It's the breath. Not enough breath. Gradual and general slackening. I've got to change rhythm. Start again from scratch. Exercise.

The smell of tools creates the ideal atmosphere for the serious consideration required to save this family from inescapable logistical ruin.

They're done for unless I act fast. Make major improvements in their well-being invisible to the naked eye. They'll never know a thing. They'll put it down to the food *delicious truly extraordinary.* They'll feel so much better. It's progressive. They'll be more relaxed. Like astronauts who change their blood on the return trip from Jupiter.

But that's not what I'm here for.

I can't forget that; I must remember that I'm here to do something bigger than all of us.

And the best way to hide this secret project from them is to forget it myself. You can't be blamed for an unpremeditated act.

And to facilitate forgetting, get very, very busy.

Don't change diet or habits.

Don't indulge in fantasies.

Build a model of the house in order to work out the servants' every move. I could easily find a plan of the facade down in the archives to ascertain its exact height. I could measure a tree by multiplying the length of a rod held up before my eyes by the number of steps that separates me from it.

But how to do this with a table covered with documents that can't be removed for fear of being caught in the act.

If one is in service.

Establish an exercise field in which an assistant lines up pre-measured standard objects so I can practice rapid estimation. Water jug 6 inches, sideboard 67 inches, beam 147 inches, Douglas pine 1339 inches. Pretty soon I walk into a room and click: armoire 84 inches.

In a single glance.

I use molded paper designed for model trains to represent the rocks, green felt for the fields, and wax, which I mold and paint, for the furniture.

From above, the house is a battlefield on which little figurines carry out troop movements.

I consider these movements carefully, their

frequency, timing, and priority, and then I record them using lines of varying thickness and color, giving each one its appropriate abbreviation: CGOL (carry glass from office to library).

The resulting diagram has the odd quality of an x-ray – first you see the bones, then the liquids that course around them, and then the working molecules in the background.

I could simply photograph all the furniture, then cut out each piece and glue it in place on the model, but how can you justify photographing a wall with two tables and a commode? Unless it happens to be the little girl's birthday.

If the little Miss would stand right there, please.

Whyyyyy?

It'll make such a lovely photo. That's right, just there.

Whayere?

Right there. Good. How pretty you are. The dress is perfect. It's D–Day.

I then prepare a background ruled off in

regular, numbered squares in order to facilitate the precise placement of each object. It's a problem of personal conscience.

And there you have it, dear friends: my project. I sit down before the mirror.

Tape recorder: Click. Play.

A commode, for example; I shall take the example of a commode.

And so my dear Sirs, this is not just a piece of furniture of which one must consider the style (oooooh!), the material (repairs and finish), the encumbrance (how to avoid it), the contents (how and for whom to arrange them), no, no my good Sirs, it's a true mystery if you analyze the ancient dust hiding behind the drawers. You'll find a potpourri of desiccated fibers, disintegrated hairs, and carpet molecules, all transported there by involuntary pollination.

I pronounce those last two words with a slightly vibrato.

This is a place that no one has ever seen, nor ever will see, with the exception perhaps of some future woodworker who won't give a second thought to the amazing provenance of this dust. It's marvelous.

The last step is to anchor the model to a sturdy plank, rigged to an ingenious system of pulleys so that the whole thing can be automatically whisked up to the ceiling at the slightest intrusion. Routine inspection will discover nothing.

Still, the rolls of green felt, blocks of modeling wax, workbench covered with sawdust, solder, and photographic enlargements of family members could be rather shocking to someone just stumbling upon them.

Repeat before sleep: I am here to do something precise.

Say it out loud.

Distill entire program into mnemonic terms and basic images to keep it dormant but always readily available in memory.

For instance, if I need to remember my name, I just think of a cage. The one in the eye exercise at the ophthalmologist's, the one the bird flies into and then back out of whenever you squint.

Squint now:

★　[ ]

15

The microbe I caught is multiplying fast. It must be a virus because I was fine just seconds ago. Then poof!

I knew the guest was a doctor because he keeps strange equipment in his room. An operating theater that folds out like a camping-trailer. A lamp with a green shade on the desk, a narrow cot.

Knock, knock.

My natural defenses are shot, I tell him as I walk in.

Rose bacteria? Swamp virus? A rusty nail, you name it – dirt behind a stone, infected animal remains, that's all it takes.

I must not have been paying attention – it's my fault, really, I add, picking up the dirty glasses from the night table. He doesn't answer, just keeps on reading his foreign newspaper.

Or else it's a chemically-derived microbe,

the consequence of abnormal temperature or of rotting swamps stewed up to a mini–hell. It could be that.

Within any current illness lurks an earlier one. For instance, if you pass samples of healthy skin under a microscope, you'll find them riddled with old traumas just biding their time.

I'm sure there's a code that hides deeply buried scars in one of my DNA sequences. That's the real cause of my present malaise.

My breathing conceals inner sighs. Internal scars float up to the surface in a random whirlwind of yes/no sequences. Dead electrons swirling in the void.

I climb up on a chair in order to attract his attention. But he keeps on reading. Except that no one could really be reading with all the racket I'm making.

It's simply a flurry of useless cells disrupting muscular efficiency. It's like pouring coffee into a radio. I've got a bad hand. It doesn't work like it used to.

I get down on my knees to look under the

bed. There's a forgotten shoe way at the back. I slide under, still talking.

I hear too loudly, that's the problem. It's terrible.

I'm slowing down. I drop things all the time. I forget names. I see everything in black and white.

But it's weird – since I've been talking to you I've suddenly started seeing in color.

It's extraordinary. I've never seen in color before. All this grey dust back here is marvelous.

There are gaps in the words, [ ]s and [ ]s, and I don't know what to do.

What is there in a [ ]?

The real problem is that I hear too loudly. I can't adjust the level. I need to be re-adjusted.

A bouquet of yellow tulips pressed up against my face gets deeper and deeper yellow because the sun goes down, Doctor. Everything emanates its accumulated light, like long-dead stars that still shine. Darkness, though deferred, is right behind.

The shoe is only an inch away now. I stretch my hand out as far as I can, my mouth filling with dust, I'm making progress. I have to raise my voice louder and louder because the mattress muffles the sounds.

The virus is clearly well hidden deep down in my vigorous health.

Like someone who has dark circles just beneath the ruddy glow he got from sitting in a patch of sunlight in the waiting room.

At least that's what I think, I tell him, gingerly extracting myself from the dust-nest, shoe in outstretched hand.

— *What on earth are you talking about?* taking off his steel-rimmed glasses, revealing a red mark on his nose. It's like his glasses were painlessly sinking down to the bone the way a ring buries itself in a finger. I'd advise him to change his glasses, but I don't have the nerve, not to mention that I'm flat out on my back and he's just forced a six-foot plastic, greased-up tube with a camera at the end down my throat – its descent filmed and projected live onto the ceiling where there's a screen ten feet square. It's the first time I've ever seen my insides in color. *You haven't got a thing, not a thing, you're sound as a bell.*

I get up, pull out the tube and whip it, lasso-like, around his neck, then tie a good knot at the camera end, which is filming his bright red, bulging eyes and projecting them onto the big screen. A thread of saliva trickles out between his already-lavender lips, followed by a thin stream of blood + rapid tapping of frantic foot. With my right hand, I drive a scalpel into his thigh.

— *You've got nothing at all. You're perfectly fine,* opening his newspaper with a quick snap, extracting a cigarette from a red enamel case adorned with a miniature black cat's head, meticulously packing it down with little thwacks of his fingernail against the cork tip.

There's got to be something that can get that yellow out. It sinks into the fingertips like indelible ink. Does the same to the stucco moldings and angels; you've got to get them clean as a whistle before repainting them, scrub them down with Clorox or Saint Mark, do it right.

Saint Mark, yes, yes, that's the ticket. Reread Ch. II, v. 28. Remarkable.

I make my way to the door like a sleep-walker. No doubt about it, I'm sick.

16

I'm short of breath. I've got to exercise more often. I'm tired, I'm useless, I'm not progressing. I'm dust in the dust. I've got to get in shape. I run along the river in a bright orange running suit beneath the pale sun.

Isn't it beautiful / Isn't it beautiful I repeat each time my stride doesn't quite reach the required 6.5 feet. The azalea and liquidambar bushes splash spots of bright red against the homogeneous background of the meadow. Got to go all the way, huh? I cry again. Next, you'll have me hauling sacks of stones.

Yep! he indicates with a sign. The only hint of effort is a single drop of sweat on his cleanly shaved head. We're going to make a stone-breaker out of you, a steer-wrestler, a piano mover.

Yep.

Eighth time we've passed those huge bushes. They're making those bright red splashes across that homogeneous green background more than ever. Tenth time. Now you're going to sing. Sing "If my aunt had had some / O-ay – o-ay / She would have been my uncle / O-ay – o-ay."

There's a margin of error in every calculation, I explain to them while we take a break and sit panting on the logs in the clearing.

We've got to reduce that margin to the absolute minimum. It's our job to take precautions. When a guy tells you *I wanted this like that, there's been some mistake, I wanted tea not coffee*, no doubt about it, he's already in the enemy camp.

Today, you have to think upstream of the situation. You could say that things that haven't been invented haven't been invented because they're not needed.

True?

– *True*, says the butcher's assistant like an automaton.

NO, I scream. Novelty is always needed.

– *Nov-el-teee*, chants the electrified group in chorus.

Prepare a list of all the new services in

case the occasion for a little demonstration arises. Give each one a name, show that though they're designed for specific situations, they're fully adaptable to any circumstance, just like printed invitations where all you have to add is what?

Silence.

A date and a name in the appropriate blanks, I scream.

Example, suppose I've planned a rabbit for luncheon. It must be raised on seasonal wild grasses in a clean hutch. Why?

Because it's cleaner, replies the bootboy.

No, I scream. To improve the race. By raising them in maximum hygiene, progress is made. By selective breeding, you can get blind rabbits that think of nothing but eating. Which is how we came up with the idea of Basement Hutches.

Who came up with that one?

– *I did*, replies the chauffeur, a real genius.

Excellent. I'd thought of it too. This coincidence is one more proof that it's a great idea. It's from repeated examples that one forges the truth. To top it off, the humidity gives the flesh a slight taste of saltpeter, which artificially replaces the usual curing and allows us to have Instantly Edible Rabbits on hand at all times. Remarkable.

What do you do when the rabbit is dead?

Silence.

First, skin it, beginning with a cut between the back feet. Then insert your hand to enlarge the opening. Break the bone of the thigh above the knee. Cut off the feet. Pass the feet out through the hole made at the beginning. Dislocate the upper thighs and turn back the skin by pulling it towards the head to finish the job.

You nail the living animal onto an inclined plank, head held in place by rubber bands tied inside an air chamber. Several planks, several rabbits ready and waiting whenever needed. A veritable traffic-jam of pillories.

— *What you gain on the one hand, you lose on the other*, drones the chauffeur.

Absolutely. He's fantastic.

Another example. Prepare a given situation, and, by "forced-choice," make the enemy take the desired role. Come up here George, I say to the chauffeur.

Stand there. Very good.

"George Brings M His Paper." We're going to play that scene. You be George, naturally (laughter), and I'll be M.

Off we go. I mime the opening of the doors. Go on George.

— *This world we live in — there's something, what's the word, atrocious about it don't you think?* says George in an obsequious voice, handing me the newspaper. *If milord will permit me to say so. Death on every page.*

Very good. Typical response from M: *What the hell are you going on about George?*

I manage a rather good imitation of his voice.

Or, a possible variation, I could say instead: *That's enough George, just bring up tonight's menus!*

Or: *"Atrocious" why do you say "atrocious," George? That's just life.*

I imitate him, heaving a sigh and opening the paper with a snap.

In all three cases, George must come back with "Atrocious Sir." It's tough to do that "Atrocious Sir." Let me hear you say it in a truly somber voice. Go on.

— *Atrocious Sir this pervasive suffering.*

Very good. Go on. Do the whole thing.

— *This world we live in — there's something, what's the word, atrocious about it don't you think? If milord will permit me to say so. Death on every page.*

Excellent. And now M responds with something like: *Are you still whining?* Or: *The day you stop mumbling between your teeth, the world will be greatly improved.*

And now what happens?

— *George leaves,* the neophyte cries out.

No! This is just where the rest of us come in. Phase II. If there's a guest (there's always a guest), what does M do?

Absolute silence.

Let's say our guest is at the window (he's there either by discretion or boredom, right?) His eye will naturally be caught by our special tableau #234, in which you, George II, (I point to the sous-chef), are driving a yellow bulldozer, while in the scoop, you, George III (the neophyte) are standing, holding you, George IV (the bootboy) on his shoulders, armed with long-handled pruning sheers with which you are trying to cut off a dead branch 50 feet up.

And there, M, exasperated by George X, approaches the window, and seeing the guest astonished by our little group, will automatically say *They may be a bunch of clowns but they're full of good will.* Bravo George.

That is the Art of Domestic Organization. It's the latest technique. Supple, flexible, adaptable to the ever-changing desires of the customer. And the customer is always right. Maximum care-taking production, faithful adherence to Dr. I-feel-good-in-the-morning. Good luck Gentlemen.

Off we go. Last exercise – exit gracefully with a plate on your head and your two hands tied behind your back. Hopping on one foot. Just kidding.

17

I run. I don't run fast enough. 500 yards. Bright and early – my time of day.

I've to work out, I've got an important job to do. I have to be in shape. 1 mile. I pass in front of the memorial *La morte avalé par la victoire*, engraved, which translates into something weird like death is wallowing in victory.

What victory? What death? Wallowing where? 2 miles. Off to the sides it's all deep, deep green. 2.5 miles. Going down into the valley, zip. Green, green, green mottled with the pale tan of the path through the grass. 3 miles. Chapel. *And the Lord told him you are nothing* screams a guy in black arms raised on the other side of the illuminated windows.

> *What did God say?*
> *he said go down into the garden*
> *you'll see this and that*
> *all right then <u>this and that</u> I made it all*

God said do it in memory of me
so go on do it

But if on the contrary God doesn't add
don't do it in memory of me
by all means don't do it

And if God says nothing at all and adds nothing
do nothing
do nothing at all

What lord? 3.5 miles. Dip down into the black hole where all the grass is dead. Ex maria virgines. Heading down toward the water. Et homo factus est. I can still hear them singing.

Ex what?

Little groves of beeches. Crackling dead leaves and twigs underfoot. 6 miles. Arcing through the woods toward water and moss.

What does God say then?

When you're almost there.

Breathe stretch legs. When it's done (he's seen you that's good) don't think of anything focus on for example "the beautiful land-scape" say: I walk along flex breathe I walk along.

When it's over you have to forget that he's seen you. Focus again on the beautiful land-scape stretch legs one arm two arms breathe in yes flex that's it forget about it. He's happy and so are you.

Slipping sideways down to the ford, and before I know it, I'm there.

Morning coolness + stimulating quantity of oxygen from photosynthesis = fish. Shhh.

Stop and no noise. Crawl forward. Vision polarized to facilitate view straight to river-bottom.

Black eye, second dorsal fin reduced and tinted orange, powerful caudal fin, body cov-ered with between 110 and 125 small scales.

I cast the plastic mayfly several inches up-stream. The slight splash as it lands on the water mimics that of dinner falling from the overhanging foliage. Thanks to a quick back-ward snap of the rod's tip at the exact mo-ment it lands, it arrives precisely at ten o'-

clock so to speak. As soon as I pull back on the lure just a hair, he'll go for it. I must compensate for the sudden weight on the line by a brief slackening or else it'll break.

But something warned him – a sound or maybe even the shadow of the line itself. So long.

Or maybe it was my shadow. Or maybe it was the cloud I thought was perfectly canceling out my shadow. A cloud that went by too fast leaving me exposed. In full sun. Damn.

What if someone saw me? All alone in front of an empty pond. Just sitting here, 95 degrees out, hair a mess, wearing a dark, heavy suit, half-hidden in the grass – how must I look?

But they can't see me. I've dug a trench, like you would for duck-hunting. Practically made a house of it, with a woodstove, piles of cushions, gas lamp, tartan covers, tunafish sandwiches, hard-boiled eggs, etc. All the books neatly arranged in a bookcase with, if it isn't too long, a hand-written summary of the story.

For instance, a man talking about his childhood happens to drag a piece of cake through his tea, and suddenly he remembers his entire past, perfectly intact – not reduced to a single phrase, like it'll be when you're dying, but in real time. So you find yourself dealing with someone who's saying very slowly that he's telling you his memories really fast. Or vice-versa.

One morning, a man finds himself transformed into a cockroach or a giant rabbit. Naturally, his whole family is horrified, but they continue to treat him as a thinking being – he doesn't come out of his room much anymore, they say, things seem to be getting worse, etc.

A man decides to leave his native country and is shipwrecked. As soon as he's established the minimal conditions for existence, he launches into more and more elaborate and unnecessary projects until he becomes a saint without knowing it.

I read through my summaries. As warm in here as the inside of a sleeping elephant.

They can't see me, that's the main thing. The trapdoor that covers the hole is disguised by a layer of grass.

I'm at the bottom.

I'm two fish behind glass, oval and curved, hanging out in the attic. I'm a crack in the parquet filled with crumbs. I'm tasteless and colorless.

I'm a molecule that belongs to the chair on which I'm sitting; *I destroy bad memories,* the air does not come from above but from all the little pores in the breathing earth. I'm far below with the roots of the irises. The belly inside the field. Muscle–fibers in a slice of ground. Meat of self in moss of earth. Little block of natal–gray. That's how I see it.

It's beautiful.

Everything is in everything. It's marvelous, *I destroy bad memories,* like the trout swallows the fly. I'm here and I'm staying.

18

The woman who always sits at the end of the table – I've been aware of her for a while now.

The first time, I was trying out a new telescope and tripod, and she kept walking past my camouflaged personnel–surveillance post. A redhead with a big nose and big feet. Always chasing butterflies or looking into anthills or dangling her legs in the cistern as soon as it's over 80 degrees.

I happened to have attached a camera to this telescope, which made each enlarged molecule of her face look like a blurry grey spot. You'd have to gather up the whole collection and put it way off in the distance before you'd recognize anything.

Her freckles are like bees or like the sun on grass filtered through the leaves or like ants on a pear, or bugs in a salad.

With the heat, these freckles must ferment and produce an abnormal warmth, like a devouring fever within the earth, or a piece of meat hung on a wall, or a pound of buried plums, or a rabbit head in a cupboard, or a sausage behind a dresser.

I will have her.

I inch along hugging the wall not daring to breathe lest I set the aspic trembling.

I enter.

— (…) *my own studies of the speakers of a certain number of languages indigenous to the north of Ghana, well, what I mean to say, is, well* (…)

I walk up to the sideboard with the big covered platter, the one that looks like it must be hiding the cooked head of an enemy turned into a pig, or a wild boar, or a cow. Reminds me of those pies with doves hidden in them or cakes full of sirens. Seems the speaker has thought of this too because he stops speaking and stares at the reliquary–pillory.

Quick check. She's there. It's definitely she.

She's even more beautiful in reality. Perfect freckles.

I see her in color.

I love her.

– (…) *leads me to similar conclusions,* perseveres the voice that I now identify as that of the cousin. *The idea of blackness is associated with darkness, while that of whiteness is inoffensive. They think like we do (…) which ought to make us admit, nonetheless, that there do exist traits of a collective consciousness. QED.*

– *We find that most reassuring,* says M, ironic in the face of a lengthy discourse on something he'd already thought. *I can't stand sociologists and psychoanalysts who tell you that deep within a cat is a cat in order to explain that a cat is a cat,* he says in a low voice to Guest II on his left (red sauerkraut, electric blue suit, day–glo heels) who doesn't get what's going on because she doesn't understand spoken English.

I offer Guest I the platter with poached beef in Stilton sauce, reconstructed down to every detail of the animal on a 12/100 scale.

– *Marvelous! this [ ]?* the artist–in–residence tentatively begins.

Poached beef in Stilton! cries out Guest IV (male, decoration, glass eye) to show that he knew it right away and that furthermore he finds the question quite out of place (art. 415: never speak of the food while at table).

But how can you keep from mentioning the very thing you're doing?

P-OA-ch-ed, insists M, also registering disap-proval of this conversation, which goes on and on. At the same moment, our artist (scarred face, smallpox no doubt, clothes too large) grabs his fork and skewers the two slices of beef he's been visibly coveting.

— *I love it!*

— *One can truly love only God,* replies a man at the end of the table who's so far never said a word.

— *What incredible dogs, eh!* says M, intercept-ing a more interesting conversation going on nearby.

— *Eeencredeebul!* cries Guest VII (wig and false mustache, dyed). *Zee eeencredeebul great dogz!* cough, cough, choke, choke.

— *Racing dogs, not hunting dogs. No, no, I cate-gorically RE-fuse to own one,* M goes on.

— *But zey are zoopairb!*

— *No thank you never that's enough thanks over my dead body thank you,* the last thank you weaker because it falls just as I'm serving the wine, and he doesn't want me to think that he's thanking me. *Really, better you just kill me right now,* he stands up on the table and rips off his shirt.

— *What a faaaabuuulous garden you have!* exclaims Guest VIII, Parkinson's + bad breath (even from the back).

— *I've tried to sculpt the space with masses of broom plants because they grow wild in the forests all around here,* M continues, still standing up on the table. *We noticed that the broom comprises an enormous family, from which was born, through ecological necessity, the idea of the present garden,* he declaims, one foot half immersed in the compote.

Landscape of undergrowth ruled by ferns which thrive

despite the pretty -27 degrees of this
celebrated winter
when everything died

This unendurable lesson made us all conscious
I was going to say of the notion of duration

This undergrowth surrounds the inner garden
enclosed by hedges
which surround a smaller garden
wild, untended but resonant

— *Loud-speakers amplify and broadcast the sounds of the local birds and insects,* M goes on, more pedagogical, distinctly calmed. *At first, our fauna were stupefied to hear their own sounds being echoed, but almost immediately, by instinct, they lowered their voices until they got back down to the level they're used to,* he finishes, his eyes raised, whites showing.

— *Fabulous!* says the unknown guest a bit tentatively. *F-f-f-f-abulous,* and then he whistles between his fingers.

— *Each in his place, eh? The animals have theirs,* he pursues, with a freezing glance aimed at the finger–whistler. *They're in great shape and absolutely enormous you can breathe here, it's good. It's a microclimate — we do well here; we're happy, we're at home. As a matter of principle, we don't use any chemical fertilizers, the ground is covered with mulch, humid household compost, which is pulverized, screened, and fortified with a natural algae-and-cow-manure-based fertilizer. For whatever it's worth! Nature does its part of the work, even when that work is to dominate nature.* Three deep breaths. Request for special nerve medicine. Swallows without water. Two deep breaths. *Help yourselves!*

— *Help yourself!* he repeats to the anorexic, eyes as big as saucers from the length of this speech. *No, no,* terrified by the enormous slice of beef dive–bombing her plate. *There you go. Piece o' meat, good for what ails you, though personally I think a bull is more like what you need.* Rising and holding his hands, horizontal, one over the other:

Thickness of the steak

19

14 hours 45 minutes. Coffee. Adherence striated special carpet–grip sole, slows you down on wood and tile, which can constitute a slight handicap, but changing shoes for every kind of floor gets problematic.

You can also choose a single shoe and wax it for a variable adherence, but I don't recommend it.

Approach with tray.

Dodge table. Grasp coffeepot. Pour. Suppress desire to raise pot higher and higher while pouring.

Verification of temperature: light steam on contact with cup. Heat maintained by discrete modification of coffeepot. Split it in two, coat each half with marine varnish, which acts almost like thermos glass. Slight risk of persistent smell. Put the tray down.

— *Put the tray down here.*

Between the two books? The most beautiful examples of Austrian clockwork and the monograph opened to the diagram of the excavations at Troy? I look beyond, out the window (to hide the fact that I've literally been photographing the page) in the direction of the dark mass of giant pyracantha. With a modest, absent air, to erase from their brains the fact that I just saw up close something that doesn't belong to me.

But in fact, not at all. They're talking. They've seen nothing. It's all right. Not seen, not done, I put the tray down between the two books, *she's suddenly become much less stable, you know,* says M.

*She's suddenly become
much less stable
you know*

*And it's sad
to see her like that
even so*

*She's losing her strength
I told her
do whatever you want, old girl*

It'll do you good
if you don't, you'll never get over it

The human being
simply demands
a certain dose of [ ]

Reserved people don't
how can I put it
necessarily do very well

I work it out
it's like saying
spinach is good
for people who are sterile

Parentheses
someday I'm going to write down
everything I eat at one sitting
Especially the giblets

But her, she made a huge mistake
you've got to admit that with a handicap like that
no way around it it's rough

— *That reminds me of what the guy at the garage told me*, the unknown guest interjects, trying to give an added touch of veracity to M's pontificating. *He said "How about Madame Duc."*

— *Ha, ha, ha,* howls M. *How about Madame Duc who lives in the forest. Is that it? That's what he's on about?* looking at our guest like a human being for the first time.

How about Madame Duc who lives in the forest
they took a look at her intestines
chock full of cancer

That's why with me
they don't look at my intestines
said the mechanic.

20

Now, all I have to do is coax the redhead into my room under some pretext or other. I'd like to show you the cases in which I've saved various family treasures, organized by number.

Through the door just there. Waaaattch your head. Good. Go on in.

In fact, I had randomly gathered all sorts of little trinkets and hidden them in the invisible kangaroo pouch sewn into my deftly cut uniform. Snippets of cloth and torn clothing, trimmings from hair cuts, samples of handwriting, gift paper, stamps, disintegrating butterflies' wings, spare change, spent candles.

They've recently discovered that Pompeii was nothing more than an encampment of bums and vagabonds at the time Vesuvius erupted, I'll tell her as I flick on the indirect lighting at the foot of the display cases.

The reclaimed objects were already recycled objects.

Like a race–car turned into a henhouse.

Look at this photo.

That's what I'll tell her first.

You must be hot? No? You're all right? We move on to classification, *her freckles are larger up close*, it's not organized by date but by degree of disintegration. Here's an egg, and here's what it becomes in six months, in twelve stages. And here's what happens to a fingerprint from the nineteenth century when exposed to the air, and here's another one, kept in a vacuum. Incredible, isn't it?

Sure you're not too hot? No? Perfect. Here, so to speak, we witness the Work of Time on private life. With emphasis on the f + almost audible "silent" e. Without the protection of dust, fat, ashes or lava.

Jostle her "accidentally," falling against her so as to touch her breasts, scent = so much % of and so much % of. Temperature = X degrees. Consistency = so much +/– elasticity. Sensation of bones below = ?

Fall asleep under the onslaught of emotion.

Wake up naked. Sodomy. Double penetration, finger in the anus + fellatio, licking feet, biting thighs, etc.

We'll do it all.

To prepare for this visit, I must organize the display cases by collecting various discarded objects, steal one or two here and there to hurry things along. Who's ever going to notice the disappearance of a pencil, a collar–button from a spare shirt, or a scrap of used blotting paper?

Operation Freckles.

Closer and closer together toward the bridge of her nose.

Eyes blackbird–black.

Voluntary silence interspersed with moments of great volubility.

— *Eeeees eeeeet eeeees eeeeet you zeeee gagagardenair?*

Shovel in one hand, rake in the other, reply ready: <u>Yes</u> and what's more I'm going to show you something. Find the mistake, I'll say to her, as I lead her top speed across the main pathway, turn to the right, path Z to the left, tip–top speed.

She's flying along horizontally like Peter Pan's sister, streaming through the sky as if an airplane door had suddenly opened.

To land in front of a bed of white roses, in the middle of which I've placed a single red one.

Find the mistake.

— *Eeet's eeet's eeet's zeee red one.*

And then I say something like: Very Good Yes Yes Very Good. It's just like you, a Mys–tery within this Ocean of Banality, and just when she blinks her eyes in surprise, I grab her by the waist, pull up her blouse, and maul her breasts and ass a little. She gets down on all fours just as a small group walks into the greenhouse, *got to fix that broken pane there*, looking over at me with a start, *what the hell are you doing down there?* Looking at me questioning black eyebrows coming together + dark rings = eyes of dead owl.

21

I go running whenever I have the time. Gradually, my movements get more supple. Hands fanned out to push back the wind. The layer of fat around my muscles moves in rhythm like the folds of aspic around a chicken.

Behind me, little clouds of dirt rise up rhythmically like those that a horse makes running across sand. *I destroy bad memories.* That's how I see it.

Running is good.

I breathe in through my teeth like you should. I flare my nostrils to increase the intake of oxygen, which, thanks to all the stored up nutrients, combines with the nitrogen in my body. The complex sugars are time-released at the ideal rate for their use. I'm in great shape.

I'm tired. 9 miles. I'm slowing down. My respiration is unfortunately limited by the narrowness of my esophagus. This strangulating channel restricts the intake of fresh air filled with positive particles, which would increase my capacity tenfold. Under normal conditions.

But not under these.

Certain deep tissues are not getting sufficiently irrigated. Risk of definitive blockage. *You're going to stay like that forever.* Permanent ringing in the ears. Eternal trembling of the eyelid. Temples crushed like the two Gs that I will feel at the command of the plane that striates the sky precisely at the point that the shadow of the tip of the poplar becomes aligned with that of my hand. Tango Zulu leader. Hallelujah I run. My name is anyone. X Y Z?

I let out the throttle. Huge strides across the grass. Leaping over the walnuts of the giant squirrel. Paw as claw for tearing into soil. Bird in the middle of the sky. Ex-tapestry click-clack in the open blue. May X bless you.

There is a zone of unknown suffering. 15 miles. Why must I say yes? I do too much. There's no reason for it. I disperse the rest of the available nitrogen into my most distant muscles. Pollens and poisons filtered from the outside air that's all right. I rhythmically crush tiny clods of earth beneath my feet. The nutrients I stored up this morning give me sufficient range.

It'll be all right.

Everything bad is being transformed into good. I immerse myself in the carpet of dense green grass. I burst forth again along the line I've laid out for myself.

It's marvelous.

But I'm a little bit tired. 20 miles. It's not like clockwork. Like it should be.

I'm hearing things.

Like a door banging in an attic. Someone unrolling a coil of wire. Someone kicking a piece of sheet-metal. A wave hitting a plastic bucket.

Let's go home.

22

Today will be harder, I tell them, Phase II. You want to make progress?

Dead silence.

You think it's enough to listen at keyholes and overhear a thing or two in the hallways?

— *We could hide under the tables* the new guy suggests.

Hide under a table. Great idea. Stunning. Just try it. In no time you'll be hearing *Where's George?* from above.

And if they should happen to get the bright idea of looking under the table to see if the foot-bell is broken? Bravo George.

There's a better way to find out what they really think. Reconstruction. It's statistically proven. If I say, adopting the Standard Guest Voice, *The weather's perfect but tomorrow there will be (…)?*

There will be (…)?

— *News!* cries the boot-boy.

A storm you idiot! I get up and pop him

one so hard it knocks him off his chair; head cracks on table going down.

Fill in the blanks for yourselves. By accumulating information against a minimal margin of error. Moral: We Must Communicate. We live in a society that suffers from a deficit of communication.

That's where I got the idea. A newspaper. The Daily Internal and Confidential News. Covering everything that the Quality thinks, supports, and wants. Every evening: paper produced after-hours – which means, off-the-clock (considering that, thanks to this new rag, you'll be saving no end of time, it's really a great deal).

Working more in order to work better equals?

– *Working less*, cries the chauffeur, thrilled to be grasping it all. And there we have it – a mere man with the stride of a giant. I'd trade him against all the others any day. He's got brains, moral sense, and a truly panoramic vision. But we're not going to give him a raise right away. Better to let him think he's still got a lot to learn so he keeps up his momentum.

I continue drawing on the blackboard. If Daughter X has just had a miscarriage brought on by the rage of her future father-in-law, it is titled "Miscarriage." And we deduce from a rapid turn around the table in which everyone expresses himself freely, the possible consequences to the menus, the cleaning schedule, the restocking of the bathrooms, etc.

It'll all be in the paper. Everything explained, with detailed drawings. Everyone can speak freely. You can dare to say what you really think. Everything's out in the open.

It's going to work like a charm.

23

The rabbit leaps from a clump of standing asparagus. The fur on his back made of artichoke fibers dyed with raspberry vinegar, a real carrot between his teeth. Eyes, two red currants.

The conversation continues, getting touchier and touchier.

— *What d'ya mean "noble Savages!" Are you completely mad! Ok, ok, just compare one of your friends' tunes with a well-written choral piece! Go ahead! Let's see!*

— *No, you're quite wrong there,* says the unknown guest who's feeling once more the bitterness of his earlier rebuffs. *It's all wrong, I tell you, utterly, entirely wrong,* straight into M's adamantly negative face.

— *You idiot.*

— *Now, now, ha, ha, temper, temper,* says the reckless unknown.

M rises, gets up on the table, hauls him up

by his collar, repeats three times *want to see my temper?* and plunges the carving knife into his chest. A jet of dark blood pours out onto the tablecloth.

I was hoping he'd do it.

Do it.

I can influence him at a distance. He knows I'm watching him; mentally, I stick pins into his wax effigy, *pass me the sauce*, he says. He gets it. It's a code; he's telling me to pass him the knife; he's going to kill him.

If he doesn't do it, I will; pardon me, just go on ahead if you don't mind, dark corridors, etc. Watch your head! This way. Be careful of the steps there wham!

— *Ethnocentrism / regressive / even so you might want to re-read… /* continues the repetitive cousin, getting progressively more terrified.

— *Serve yourself, don't be shy, old fellow, take the head, that's the best part, yes, yes, go on, it's already cut off. And you my dear,* turning to address the anorexic, *take the tail, that piece there, with a bit of horseradish it's really quite good, thaaat's it.*

I pass the vegetables counterclockwise.

Cabbage and turnips in minced brains. The cousin resumes his dissertation on myth.

— *Which are not myths in the sense that we're used to. Such as the Unicorn or Pegasus. Rather, they're schemes of perception closer to our usual sensations, such as hot and cold, raw and boiled, burned, or rotten.*

— *Moral:* screams M, *if I want to piss, excuse me, is that a myth?*

— *For the Baramabaratamaras, to bury their dead without a stone on their feet is an absolute taboo. It's to remind them that the sea once covered the earth and that it could do so again.*

— *Enough,* screams M.

— *The same is true of phobias,* continues the cousin, head lowered.

— *Phobia of what if you please?* screams M.

— *It's simple,* says the unknown guest, who's been trying to get a word in. *There are two types of anxiety. The 1st is automatic, and there's nothing you can do about it. The 2nd is called "signal anxiety," and its function is to deflect the 1st; therefore, it's an economical anxiety — something that's bound to interest you.* He gets up and throws his glass against the wall.

— *If the signal anxiety isn't working*, he continues in a "mad scientist" tone, *the automatic anxiety develops unchecked and passes into Phase II, a state of permanent distress*, he gets down on one knee, *self-deprecation, uncontrollable acts*, he pantomimes a strangulation, *ritual murder, human sacrifice, uncontrolled kidnapping.*

He ties his napkin around his head like a pirate and runs around the table flailing his arms. *Loss of the transitional love object, neurotic sense of destiny, escape into madness, hyper-fluidity of libido, perversion of maternal instinct, irrepressible urinary eroticism, need for punishment, infinite return of the primal scene, and from there — bon voyage.*

Utter silence.

— *That's what it's like, believe me. No way around it*, he adds into the silence. He sits back down. *That exactly how it happens, I swear it. That's it.*

— *Who told you so?* asks M.

— *I read it in a book about the man who discovered the [ ] and in [ ] uh you know the book. What is the title of the thing? You know, the one where there are all these people in a house and by the end, zero, nobody left.*

Horrified look from the person at the end of the table. She's starting to feel not so good. I turn toward the dessert. I'll save her. It's as good as done. I turn around. She gives me a sign—a little wink. That's the signal.

You just have to pay attention.

She's on my side. I know it. I'm going to save her. We'll escape together. We'll run away across the fields. We'll outsmart the dogs. We'll walk along through the stream to destroy our scent.

White skin not used to sun.

You'd better cover yourself. Here, take this, handing her some sort of animal skin. Discretely help her as she undresses in order to take a census of her freckles.

File it away in the memory.

Goose–pimples. *I-I-I'm c-c-c-cold.* No, no, really, just keep on going you'll see it's really nice up ahead. All sorts of botanical mutations and surprises around here – it's a downright miracle. The branches fall any which way, hit this acid soil and, poof! before you know it, they're right back to growing again. The jungle is built of spontaneous grafts, take that way there, that's right, beeeee caaaareful of the thorns. Goooood.

The plants, not being used to the sun, take on a walloping dose of vitamins and suddenly pow! they're off and running.

Barring viruses, that is, which also, of course, in their own way, serve to strengthen them.

— *V-v-v-v-viiiiruses???*

Yep, I tell her, in–dee–structible viruses. And therefore: carnivorous plants. Why? Well, taking her by the chin and looking at her squarely, because nature's like that, it's just like that, that's what it's like, look, you're tired, you're hot, your eyelids are getting heavy. Lie down. That's right.

It's a space blanket. Mylar.

Don't move an inch. I'm going to gather wood for a fire. What? I've got my hatchet, look, special – double–bladed, like Clovis'. Chop! one side and then chop! the other. I'll be back.

If you see red ants don't move. The trick is

to stay absolutely still. After a minute or two they start thinking they're on a dead log and they move on. Hold on now, just get a little closer to the fire. We'll have to camp here tonight. I know, I know, but that's just the way it is.

In case of danger, it's necessary to recreate a hierarchy. Just remember your classics. There has to be a leader. Number 1, that's me. I stare down at my steel–tipped boots. I know it's my strongest argument. That's why I'm already on top of her, lying across her body, my hand in between her thighs to hold her in place and kissing her. A thread of spittle gathers at the corners of our mouths. *For me, it's quartets* brings me up with a start.

— *Me too, chirps a frail little man, everything I love is in a quartet. I told you, did I not, that my father was a doctor? Well, with him it was symphonies. My uncle said to him: that's music for the gut. I can still hear him saying: But you, with your silly minuets, your limp little ditties, your frills, you amuse me.*

— *He had a point*, the unknown guest sticks in, still pushing his luck, *after all, it's symphonic* art that prefigures the modern abstract movements that followed. Specifically in its monochromatic aspects, I should add. Repetitive, minimal, economical.

Silence.

— *That reminds me of an evening. Knock, knock. Who's there? A very well-know organist,* M cries out, *good god what was his name? Caesar? Médor? Radar? Doesn't matter. Anyway, Radar was blind. No problem, they played, four hands, dinner. We went back with him to his room, he walked in and said: Thank you so much for bringing up my bags. He knew instantly simply from the change in the acoustics that his suitcase was in the room. Now, that's an ear! And to top it off, he was always happy, always funny, always saying "I saw" or "I see that…" or "I see, I see." Really marvelous.*

— *That reminds me of one of my men who had an amazing sense of humor,* adds the unknown guest, *one day we're up in the air and the guys down below start firing like at Gravelotte. Bang! they hit our right engine, and my navigator, one of our boys from the Second Zouaves, turns to me and you know what he says? Just like that he says, So long, Colonel. Today everything's changed. You start to understand why our veterans are so bitter.*

    — *The human being,* interjects the woman with the gold teeth, *no matter what, remains capable of noble actions. Certainly, of course. But then two years later you read in the newspaper that this same saint has shot his entire family before "Turning the Gun on Himself." So give me a break with your fond memories of war. You piss me off.*

    — *What?*

    — *You heard me — you piss me off. Want it written out and signed, Colonel?*

    — *Finish up that rabbit,* barks M, *there's a carrot hidden in the bullet hole — whoever finds it first, wins.*

24

Night 4 miles. Hyper–oxygenation of brain due to increased flapping of arms. Today I'm racing along. 12 miles an hour. I'm doing fine. 37 strides/minute. I'm the insect with steel wings, the flying scarab. Paper fly, bone machine, *finish up that rabbit finish up that rabbit.* Put calf ligaments 422 into action.

Accelerate, then breathe.

Run.

5 miles. Blindly descending toward the sound of black water. Dive–bomber into the black. Dwarf slipping between the black grasses. Batman, that's me. My cape deployed like wings *I'll escape this nightmare,* I'm a bird cheep–cheep I'm a scurrying mouse squeak–squeak I'm both. I'm equipped with a radar that tells me where everything is in real time. I slide through touching nothing. I'm making good time.

I'm in time. 6 miles.

I am vegetal, I don't eat what the others

eat click–clack I fly.

Façades walls cracks folds.

Low–flying grass skimming machine–tool.

Remote control.

I fly therefore I am, etc.

7 miles.

I think of her, I think of her. I fooled myself. It was I who fooled myself. I didn't understand. She's a real person. Ouch. Title?

Miss?

Princess I–Regret?

You?

Invent a special dance for her. Minuet–of–Me. 10 miles. I stop to breathe. I field–dance body–cipher warnings. Arms extended in a cross = help / come get me. Standing, legs apart, one arm raised = it's ok / forget it

Seen from above, it's perfectly clear.

But I'm too small. They'll never see me. I've shrunk into nature. Wooden soldier against a wall of trees. Dwarf melted into the set. Myself lost among transparencies. You can't be everything. 11 miles. It's not so bad. I'm amazed by the sky no matter what it's doing. I'm safe no matter what happens. My shoes bounce back off the springy path. My feet make a white line across the grass. That's why I'm running. I trample the whitened grass to a pulp. I crush the white of the pulp of the trampled grass. Like jet–stream across the blue sky. But you can't be everything.

She's a real person.

I didn't realize it. It's not my fault. I should tell her. 14 miles. Blacker dark and darker black. *I didn't mean to do it.* I'm going to save her. Faster. Speed up at the end. Ooof.

I should have thought of it.

You're a real person.

I am not complete therefore I run. Every–thing resembles everything. Calves + tibias + scapulas. Everything works. Eye muscles too. It's the first time I've ever seen in color.

The black and white of the past is over.

The here and now is fabulous.

The eyes' color–cells activated. The special blood that constructs 3-D vision. The muscles of the ideas that come to you too. Everything is in everything. I run into the black water up to my neck. The displacement of the waves warns the fish. 15 miles. I have the same density as the water. Lead color + night color. But you can't be everything.

It's no big deal.

25

We've got to stop here, I explain to her as calmly as possible. That's what being a leader's all about – be reassuring, but firm. Don't listen to subalterns and their whining. That's what they get for their inexperience.

With time of course you learn how to minimizing the suffering. Too late, though, because by then you've been promoted to a less risky life.

What? You think a general stays at the front lines just waiting for a bullet? No way, he's back there in his tent, thinking things over. Stretched out on a leather couch. Or standing in front of a model of the battlefield. Like it should be done.

If he gets killed, who's going to plan the campaign?

I've got to make myself a new and much more visible uniform – got to stand out from the troops. So I can stay in my tent and fully concentrate on the next move. I never sleep. I work too much. My new uniform is red and black, plumed helmet, steel–pointed boots, life is great, I think of everything.

– *What?*

Nothing, nothing, I was just saying that we should stop here and make camp. Rest a lit–tle.

Ok, Stop. Here.

– *B-b-b-u-u-ut?* she objects.

Thought it might strike you that way – seems absurd, doesn't it? Entirely out of place, I know, but really, quite necessary for your survival. And it's an order. I repeat – it is both the privilege and the painful fate of a leader never to be understood.

And at that point, just to change the con–versation, I take out my folding walking stick and explain to her that roots and berries don't contain enough protein to keep us alive.

But luckily the temperature has reached the necessary 50 degrees, and the coolness, enhanced by the increased current, has at–tracted a swarm of bees and waterflies etc. So, fish for dinner. Worry not, I conclude.

If it's too big, we'll smoke some for pemmican.

— *For pppe-mi…mi…mi?*

Pemmican: Smoked meat or fish, ground into paste and packed into the intestine of a ruminant. So we'll have to kill a cow.

— *K-k-kill a cow?!*

The high statistical incidence of insect accidents produces a sufficient crop of cadavers per second to nourish fish to quite hefty proportions, I add just to cheer her up.

Don't look now, but right there, where the tip of that reed intersects the diagonal from that half–submerged branch, lies our fish dinner.

Watch this — I cast the line, twisting my wrist at the very end to lift the lure so that the fly lands oh–so–softly just one half–inch from the targeted spot. Not bad, eh?

With a flick of the wrist, I whip the line back over my shoulder. Just like that, see?

I maneuver the #4 Sydney special (which I've spruced up by exchanging the rooster-feather Hackle for the red and green under–feather of a male woodpecker, bound with an electric blue silk thread) into the line of sight of the fish who hears the delicate plash and finds himself staring directly at the exposed belly of a blue–bottle fly fallen from a golden bush agitated by the early morning breeze and illuminated by the glorious summer sun.

Pretty, huh?

— A-a-and wh-wh-what happens next?

The fish flicks its tail, gobbles the fly, and snaps the line.

Damn.

If you dig a canal and re–route the water, I say to change the subject as I sit down next to her, and if you line it with cement and put a vertical grill at both ends, and then install a system of adjustable louvers to increase the pressure, and then release captured fish into it, they (at least 90% of subjects tested) will resume their natural positions within a day or two.

So fishing them still counts as sport. Not cheating at all. A canal, even a small one, is not an aquarium. I slide a little closer so that my thigh just barely grazes hers. 90 degrees + shivers.

You end up knowing the fish by sight and getting fond of them, I add, appealing to her tender side.

From catching them and then letting them go. Even when their heads are above water, and even if their trembling is a symptom of stress, you can't help but wonder whether they haven't figured it out – you're not going to hurt them. I bet the air is just as pleasant to them as the water is to us – that is, if you're sure you're not going to drown dddr–rring!

– *What the hell are you doing staring at that fucking wall? I've been calling you for an hour, what the hell do you think this thing is???*"

Ooooooo dear, true, true – it's the red light, which means Library, blinking away, and so is the one for the Yellow Room. It was then that I realized all wasn't as going as planned.

26

Gentlemen, I said, turning my head. For at least ten minutes, I'd had my back to them, drawing equations on the chalkboard. We've got to get into gear. The numbers have fallen. Satisfaction is down. Heads are going to roll.

Some of you have been sacrificing the group for your personal gain, and that – that is going to stop. It's o-ver.

We're going to organize maneuvers. Any one who doesn't go along with it is out of here. Insubordination. Court-martial.

I'll admit it – I'm pissed.

— *For good reason*, interjects the chauffeur.

Thanks and fortunately you're not all to blame. All right, then. Onto the maneuvers. If you can't keep up, we'll throw you a grenade. So long.

Two groups take off into the forest. Blue against white. Bamboo cages for the losers.

— *Bamboo cages?* whines the butcher's assistant.

First slide.

Enough with trimming the hedges – we're going to do something big. We'll use an enlarged NGS map, then a stereoscopic photogrammetric restitution – that's a couple of aerial photographs off-set by about 35%, creating the impression of a relief map. The measurements were made by compass, step by step, and then transcribed.

Green and white for the forest. The darker the green, the denser the forest. Yellow parts indicate clearings where there's sunshine. The black = rocks, cliffs, houses. Though, where you're going, I'd be pretty surprised if you could knock on a door and get a bowl of soup and/or keys to the barn to catch a nap.

Blue means river. Next slide.

Brown, bumps. The slightest divot and the tiniest lump are duly noted. Not to mention the really dangerous spots highlighted in purple. You'll know if its ferns or blackberries even before you fall into them. Watch it – brambles at 10 o'clock.

You place a compass flat on your thumb.

You've got to be able to see what's coming next. Memorize the slightest trap.

Next slide. Delicate rocks.

Whites start there. Blues on the other side. Real bullets.

27

Knock knock.

No reply. Maybe he's sleeping.

I open the door, his mended vest over my arm. Hmmm, I say out loud to make myself heard through the dark. Here's your mended vest. I added a bullet-proof titanium lining. All set for the next battle. Ha-ha, I laugh.

I hear his breathing.

I grope my way across the room, heading for the bed, but ending up on the other side.

He's a doctor; he'll understand.

I've got an idea, I say out loud, I'm going to tell you all about it. I find the light switch. I flick it on. I throw myself against the desk, don his glasses, grab the paper-knife, and wait until he wakes up.

— *What time is it? What on earth are you doing? Why did you turn on the light?* Hair on end + saucer eyes. *What time is it???*

I'm not going to tell you I've got a Capricorn rising, an earth sign, with a tendency to error in the second descant compensated by a good destiny in Aquarius. No, no.

You know about electronic microscopes?

— What time is it? Are you nuts or what?

Inside the flesh you can see the molecules squirming like maggots at the bottom of a bucket. Well, it's just the same with my ideas – there are millions of little ones hiding inside the big ones – see what I mean?

Let's get to the bottom of this.

I throw myself on the carpet crawling along like a soldier. Turning at 2,000 RPM, swimming in a fireproof suit, lead boots. Parachuted into the field. I can imitate any voice. Ffffffff grass water, zzzzzzz the swamp water deep silt bamboo haak haaak bird-animals. I go down into the carpet like only I know how to do. Deep into the green and red jungle. Let's go. Onward! I can't. Leave me, comrades. I can't go on. My leg, etc. Kill me; I'll only hold you back.

Go on, kill me.

I stand up and approach the bed.

See? I point to a scar just below my knee.

See? The bullet entered through the stomach. Went through the liver, ricocheted against the shoulder blade and came to lodge itself here.

Feel this bump here?

He's asleep. He doesn't really want to wake up. His breathing's really weird, only inhaling one time out of two. He exhales twice. Inhales once.

I turn out the light.

28

And if I were to build a model of the river.

A cross-section of the water. The fallen trees in miniature. Shadows of the leaves on metallic paper. Birdsong reproduced by loud-speakers cleverly camouflaged in the margins of the sky.

It wouldn't do any good.

Or else do what the unknown guest would have done. As it must be done if one wants to be able to explain one's battles satisfactori-ly.

If, at the bottom of your heart, you want to be accepted normally into normal conver-sation.

You've got to have technique to persuade people.

Install a large, thick plank on wheels. Sculpt a landscape in relief. Cotton snow. Foam pines.

Slip on an house jacket, adjust the mono-cle, smooth down the mustache, and sit down in a veteran's wheelchair.

Off we go.

The two battalions file by in full battle gear. Braid on the jacket daffodil yellow + same color tassel at the end of the fez around which is rolled a white turban, I comment as I move my soldiers forward.

I advise using the 56/V voice with asthmatic respiration (to give it a little drama).

These admirable men execute a "superb" battle march under a hail of projectiles, shouldering their arms, as if on parade, keeping in line, tadidadidadidadida.

Meanwhile (I push the soldiers off to the side) almost immediately, there (there it is) a fusillade resounds among the underbrush.

And there fffffffffffff watttchhh outtttt fffffff booooom.

The neutron bomb, men, a weapon that is transforming the very concept of strategy.

360 degree turn.

Push the little button hidden in the left arm of the chair.

Screen unrolls automatically.

Pointer.

You can see it right here in the film, men, in such slow-motion that you'd think it's stopped (the opposite of those time-lapse films in which you see a flower blooming at break-neck speed), so the neutron bomb combines classic security with modern virtue.

Everything living is killed, but material goods are left unharmed. Absolutely untouched. The flowers in their vases, the tea in its teapot, the eggs in their cartons.

Ms. Gold-tooth would be looking at me wide-eyed *oh isn't he just marvelous!*

It would be the first time.

Pretty soon it will be my turn.

At that moment, the flag-carrier of the second Zouaves asks the colonel (that's me) who's standing behind the center of the regiment, which is to say, behind the battalion, to the left of which the flag is placed, and which is called the battalion of the flag: Colonel, is it time to mount the flag?

It's his way of saying, "Should we remove the oilcloth protecting our eagle from the rain and dust of marches and thus reveal it?"

I tell him don't bother we'll see about it later. In fact, an unfurled flag on the front lines stands out like a sore thumb. We used to do it all the time with our outmoded formations, but it's too big a risk these days when subtlety's the trick – we've got to hide our soldiers in the slightest fold of ground. Wait for just the right moment to attack.

This is no trivial matter, men, you'll see soon enough. So the flag remains furled, but with its guard close by, composed of a corporal and a dozen men.

A second later, a 120 conical–cylindrical shells falls on the highly visible group.

You've got to admit that thirteen pairs of bright red trousers makes a pretty irresistible target against a field of white snow.

My model explodes.

I crush three pine trees.

Citation: these courageous men mowed down by the shards of the iniquitous shell will remain forever as [ ]?

Victoria Cross of Fallen Summer Leaves on

Flight of Eagles.

Commander of the Theater of External Operations.

Knight Forever (in the Reserves).

Knight of the Memory of Sufferings.

Stop.

Ms. Gold–Tooth will be stunned.

I'm going to get ahead. I'll do it better next time.

I'll know how to do all the voices. The sound of the canon. I'll even do the carrier–pigeon. The ducks in the swamp. The wind in the poplars. The sound of water + the smell of honeysuckle.

I'll make the sound of walking on dry ground. The sound of the blade of grass un–folding after it's been walked on.

Crunch crunch through the snow.

Knock knock.

I go in.

Gentlemen, do you know this man?

Huge vaulted neo–Gothic hall.

Negative. (response of a group of men in uniform + cigars + cognac).

Well, he's our man.

I lisp like you've got to do if you want to get close to the truth.

The admiral. The lieutenant of the 405th. The only man for the job.

The crème de la crème.

He's our man.

Applause. Bravo.

Cheers.

I walk off down the hall.

Fade to black.

29

30 yards, hubbub getting louder, 20 yards.

Faster faster the soufflé is falling. 10 yards.

The doors open ahhh the soufflé is falling.
Voices: *Oh! it's so beeee-youuu-tiful!* they were all
set to cry out.

Disapproving silence.

The soufflé maker is a bit rebellious, laughs M
just over my head

The soufflé maker, that's me.

I admit it – at that point I cracked. I broke
into loud song to cover his voice.

Besides, my singing provided the distrac-
tion necessary to rescue a most delicate production just as a minor set-back threatened
to catalyze a catastrophe.

At least that was my reasoning.

My flawless reasoning.

The problem's not the song, but the
threshold of audibility. It's supposed to be
sung with closed mouth. The offending deci-

bels were minute compared with the increase in my service. Perfectly modulated speech, firm expressions, affirmative nods of the head so slow that they include signals invisible to the naked eye.

Pause.

And secondly, humming while serving is nothing but an "industrial accident." I therefore object to the term "professional error." Talk of "discord" or "incompatibility of attitude" if you will, but personally I'm not inclined to consider the situation in a psychological light.

Pause.

I'm useful, and here let me just remind you of but one recent incident. It was I who thought of defrosting the freezer by shooting pulverized caustic soda at it through a customized machine-gun. That idea alone, I'm sure, contributed substantially to the 60% reduction we've seen in household expenses.

Ideas like that only come to you if you can remain sufficiently detached. And such detachment can only be achieved through supreme acts of will. That insignificant song was simply one example. QED.

I have other ideas, and I'm going to take the opportunity of this meeting to tell you about them.

First, to improve security. A remote-control submarine. A landing strip with miniature hunters, armed with machine guns, ready to jump into action. With radar + vocal commands. Attack / Fire / Target # such and such etc.

If someone gets into the garden. Bam.

— *What's up with you? What are you still doing here? Have you passed out? And that soufflé, what? Saving it for tomorrow???*

I had, in fact, sort of fainted standing up. Platter in hand, my back to the sideboard, facing the big mirror. I have no idea how long I'd been standing there.

30

She comes in saying *wwwwhat is th-th-that?* It's where you are. *Whaaat?* It's a model of the house where you're staying. *Bbbbut what's it f-f-f-or?* Come look.

I imply that I'm the resident family historian. Moving discretely up on her.

Explain to her that people are always more complicated than you'd think even at the most inaccessible levels of society, with my eyes slightly crinkled + voice an octave lower to give it all a learned air.

Effect an atmospheric transformation by dimming the lights with the foot-operated rheostat.

And then, just as she's leaning over, I grab her from behind and breathe hot against her neck as I plaster myself to her buttocks and wait, whispering sweet nothings. She turns and holds me to her, opening her mouth to admit my tongue, trading saliva, sealed, her breasts pressed up against my uniform, a low groan escaping her throat, and her eyes, rolled back under the onslaught of ecstasy, hands beating, hips shaking, leaving her emptied, drained, limp on the ground, lifeless.

At first, I can't understand what's happened, lips sealed, breathing nil, no fog left on the pocket mirror. I slide her into a big plastic trash bag and bury her deep in the forest out by the generators.

No, it's ok, she's breathing.

If I say, "Now," it's already over.

Get it?

By the time I've said it, it's already passed. And so "After" can never be "Now" because it doesn't exist. And so "Tomorrow" will never again be "Before," I tell her, holding her tight.

She's astonished.

And as she opens her mouth to say something, I slip in my pre-poised tongue (that amazed her – how I managed to speak with my tongue rigid and ready to leap out of my mouth) and turn it around counter-clockwise, as it should be done, spiraling deeper and deeper.

Until it touches her tonsils, which makes her gag just as I'd planned giving me time to spin her around, pull up her dress, switch off the lamp, grab her ass in the dark with one hand, just like it should be done, and grab her by the neck with the other.

Sometimes, I add an odor of compost, or hide a piece of meat under the furniture to create a more natural ambiance. Or the sound of cows on a tape-recorder: low grunts from the stalls + panting. Pawing at the straw on the ground. Weathered door of grey wood + creaking hinges. Lightbulb swinging on its wire. Cement drainage. Low sounds recorded in the damp hay.

What-chya doing in here so late?

— *Milkin' cows.*

Flip her over in the hay. Tear off her blouse and, etc.

It's the same with the revolving map of the sky (captivating!) or the thing of recounting dreams (puts you right to sleep) or going to the exhibit: you know I paint in my spare time. *You p-p-paint?* Oh, pretty amateur stuff, of course. Last one was a triptych, "Hunt with Hare." Acrylic on wood. Come on in. It's over there. Watch out now; the door's really small. Watch your head. Too dark?

Of course it is. Wait a second. A little patience and grad–u–a–lly you'll see the painting appear, truer than nature, impression of dawn, grey, pinkish, damp meadows, etc. At first, it's a little blurry, but then it clears up. That's the idea. All of a sudden you say to yourself: it's the first time I've ever seen in color.

It's marvelous.

Make an arboreal chart of all possible strategies. Objective: I will have her. Promise: it will be good.

If that doesn't work, I'll paint her an ideal portrait of our future life together (in case she's already said yes to coming back to my place under some pretext that she's been waiting for and that I've conveniently supplied). List everything you love at the count of one. 1. Go. Don't breathe. Us, together in the little forest. Here, naked as worms, curled up in the moss in the crotch of a tree. No one will know. It's our place. *Th-th-this is th-th-th-the r-r-real l-l-l-ife,* she'll say, and off we go.

You're a real person. Pardon me. I was only trying to convince you.

I'm sorry.

— I know, no big deal. I was doing the same thing.

I know. Me too. First let me thank you for wanting it to appear real.

Bravo for the stuttering.

— I-I-I-I d-d-d-do it p-p-pretty g-g-good.

You do it extraordinarily well.

Much better than I do my imitations. Though they'd get better if I worked on them some more.

— I know.

But I'm also really good at squinting.

— Stop. Let's kiss.

I'm going to sing a little song I wrote just for you.

Yes–yes' / Oh yes' / Oh yes' / Yes–yes'

31

— *Pull! So what are you waiting for? Think that pigeon's next year's?*

I push on the handle that releases the spring, shooting the clay disk into the sky. M fires away.

— *Pull! Pull!* Two pigeons in the air.

Bam–bam, two shots of the double-barreled Browning, and the disks explode into crumbs somewhere up near the sun. *Pull!* he screams again, his face turned toward me blank black eyes staring out the demand like a monomaniacal saint.

— *Pull!* The spring of the pigeon–launch jams, so I pluck the Phillips–head screwdriver from the case hidden in my mitten, and I dive into the printed circuits of the ball-trap. Hunters shouting in the background.

The contacts are linked by soldered silver snakes that look like a hydrographic map of all my favorite spots.

Except that the scale is off, for instance the

waterfall to the right is father away, relatively speaking. *You did that on purpose, didn't you? He did it on purpose, huh?* turning to the unknown guest who's hauling two elephant guns behind him. He's hoping this means it's over.

— *Where the hell's he gone! Wouldn't you know it! What an idiot. This is nuts. What the hell are you doing in there!? Answer me!!*

I was thinking, as I crawled through the forest of electric wires, that all we'd have to do is attach a microphone to M's necktie, link it up to a loud-speaker in the office, and work out an easy-to-use code for all circumstances. "Beautiful day today" means "Change the silverware." "Oh, yes…" means "more bread." Advantage: no more foot bell or morse code (source of much error and confusion – you just can't tap six long two short one long to request a glass of water without its being spotted).

Oh yes
Beautiful day today
Blue sky

More bread! / Change the silverware! /
More vegetables!!!

Ah, such lovely flowers
Ha, ha, ha, so amusing
It's the season

Finger–bowls! / Pass the fish again! / Error
#3 (a spill! a spill!).

32

Sitting under the yellow oak in front of the impeccable carpet of the meadow. Hiding under two crossing branches. And there you have it, a true and beautiful feeling for nature. That's what I'll say on D–day.

– What?

Nature, my love, I say, tapping the bone handle of my walking stick against the polished leather of my custom–made spur–heeled boots, my free hand playing innocently with the bronze end of my .27 caliber.

You know, with this thing I could kill a 10 ton elephant charging you at 50 miles an hour.

Ah, yes, Nature.

Taking two long drags on my Panatella.

Naturally, nature produces contrary forces, which cause the sparks that some talk about too lightly as vitality.

Th-those p-p-pretty red things, what are they?

Dead leaves. Each year at the same time, the leaves fall and decay. Their last juices seep down into the pores of the earth and penetrate the deepest roots, which store up this elixir until they need it for their upward growth.

There's always a certain number of insect carcasses on the leaves, and, if you look a little closer, you'll see countless single-cell organisms. Vegetation is meat. If it weren't, how could it rot?

She likes this explanation. I must admit that I plan my pronunciation and stresses to give the words the maximum surprise. Just the way I sing Alpine beaver skin full of holes / Alpine beaver skin full of holes.

— *What?*

Nothing, just singing. I was saying that plants are meat. If not, how do you think they rot?

She's fascinated.

It's true; if you start thinking of a pine as a pile of dead cows, it changes things.

— *A p-p-pile of d-d-dead c-c-cows.*

In a manner of speaking.

I get down on my knees to demonstrate my passion.

The fish is still there, interested in nothing but maintaining his position with minimum fin-waving, fixing his eye on one spot like an anchor. 2kg 600 empty + 345 g of water taken on.

Use a hollow rod with an internal 16 pound line and an automatic reel. The right hand holds the rod at the best angle for attack while the left hand feeds out the line or pulls it back, depending on the current. The least vibration could mean a strike.

Concentration, precision, modesty, the best equipment, body kept supple and ready, eyes polarized for seeing underwater below the reflections on the surface. Steel arms, wooden legs. Don't move.

I'm alone. When you fish, you've got to be alone.

She stays in my memory.

I always remember her. I think of her.

I can bring her back at will.

The repetitive sound of a branch tapping the water's surface creates a generalized hypnotic state. The fish feel it too. I'm going to fall asleep.

Like I always do at the crucial moment.

I've got to work out more. I don't run enough. You've got to run.

I'll run all the way back.

— *What the hell are you doing there?* scream + blow of whistle.

— *Who told you could come down here?*

I say nothing.

— *Who the hell gave you the right this is an outrage* red with fury an outrage *I've never seen such a thing* really bright bright red hopping up and down in place little black suit with a badge *this is a fish preserve and you, you?*

Say nothing.

— *Who told you you could come in here? Can't you can see that it's a man-made lake? And those pumps there — what do you think they are? What you do think you own the place?*

Sitting there on the cement, 100 degrees in the sun, hair sticking out all over, dark clothes, lounging around on the grass– what must I look like?

33

If you compare the height of the rooms to that of the facade in the model, you can tell that there's space between the ceilings and floors large enough for a man to crawl through.

By slipping a folding pocket spyglass into a knot in the planks, I can get a distorted but fairly accurate view of what's going on in each room.

Example the code to the safe.

The way is clear. I open the trap door and slide back the painting of the woman asleep in her chair.

The code?

A.I.M.E. = M – pretty obvious if you know him.

A bunch of black and white photos of men in uniform, dignitaries from? And then a series taken by an itinerant photographer: a long table with diners in evening dress. M as a young man flanked by two half–naked young women. Letters in code, cards with fingerprints, sketches.

Anonymous photos.

This is my mission.

I gather up as many as I can. Go over to a chair with a lamp next to it. Replace the lightbulb with a stronger one. Take out my miniature camera, and photograph page after page, no rush, all's well, I'm a pro, I've done it so many times, I believe in what I do, they'll never know it's me because I don't know it myself.

This is my real job.

But my cover's so well developed that I sometimes forget my true mission. It's no longer a cover, it's an ostrich feather duvet.

But this is no laughing matter.

I've done it. I've accomplished my mission. I've taken all the time I needed.

I've taken too much time.

But that way no one's going to suspect me. I've done well. Exactly as planned.

I was made to compartmentalize my different activities, I'm under auto–hypnosis, all's well. Every movement timed and precise. Back erect. Eyes straight ahead. Impeccable click of the shutter at slow speed. Ear turned up to maximum receptivity. No sweat. Not a single tremble.

– What the hell are you doing there? it's M in a dressing–gown, a .32 pointed my way.

I look at him blankly and then glance down. He glances down too.

I give him a triple flying punch full in the face, then just as he's going down, I give him my right under the sternum. He's on his knees with a mouth full of blood, and I finish him off with the poker, which I wash to re-move traces of bone and hair.

Not a sound, except the scraping of pigeon feet along the rain gutters.

All is just fine, except that my hands are a little weak.

I don't work out enough.

A weak hand. Though you know it's ridiculous, the more you know it's ridiculous, the less the hand can grip what it has to grip.

I stand there for a long time, too long, I've lost my grip, I'm slowing down, I drink too much. You shouldn't drink, you should work out, I'm taking too long. Someone's going to come in.

No doubt about it and three more sheets to photograph.

Got to speed it up.

Finish the work, close the safe, replace the painting, and open up the trap door that leads to the secret passage.

34

The characteristic silver flashes refracting off the crystalline structure of his scales are visible despite his camouflage, no doubt because of the incidence of light directly overhead at noon in summer.

Vision reduced to 30 degrees in binocular view, despite the short focal length of his eye, which gives him considerable depth of field. The fish can't see me because I'm perched above him, balanced on a branch.

Because footsteps make long–wave vibrations that translate into the water as motion, which is then perceived by the sensors that operate laterally from his head, I avoid walking along the bank. As for the high frequencies, if he's from one of those families that has no eardrums, like the ventricles of carp, no problem, we can talk at ease.

I take the Hardy Perfect 3 1/8" reel out of my vest pocket. So maybe it's been superseded by other, newer models, but it remains the ideal of durability and conceptual purity – the incarnation of the perfect reel.

I install it on my special 8-foot Loomis IM6 rod of titanized carbon, and then, from my hat, I pluck the terribly realistic Cut-Wing Dun fly, parachute-shaped and the color of burnt milk.

I hold my wrist in the new "thumb forward" position and whip out the length of line necessary to span the stretch of sky separating me from my target, a blue expanse cross-hatched by ragged jet-stream. The tiny fly lands right in a natural cup formed by an eddy in the current, at the precise place and time that someone throws in an enormous stone.

— *You know perfectly well you can't fish here,* says a pale, thin man, turning toward a mustachioed colossus with stooped shoulders dressed in a shapeless black shirt and a red cap covered with decorations, a saw in one hand, a hatchet in the other, who nods his head as if to say *yeah.*

I reply that I always fish here and that this strip of river bank all the way to the dead tree up there is public property.

— *You know perfectly well you can't fish here.*

I wade across the water and tell him to repeat it. He smiles. I take a stout electrician's knife out of my pocket and plant it in his forehead.

I grab the hatchet and bury it in the other one's shoulder, and then dump them both into the water, direction eels.

Not a stone but a dead branch falling from a tree.

The shocks caused by this sudden movement enter the receptors in a millisecond, alerting the brain of the fish who raises his round eye and finds a sphere above him.

A bubble of deformed objects, huge riverbanks, gigantic waving weeds. Blazing sun overexposing one side, clouds glooming around on the other, and me, a black stem elongated by a head and an abnormal thread that doesn't have much family resemblance to a spider web. Goodbye.

35

Return to the house, exhausted as ever.

A tumult of emotions.

1. The incident with the two guys.

2. The lack of progress with the red–headed person.

3. The stolen photos.

Backache like I'd spent days in a coffin.

If I'd been in a coffin, I'd have been nourished by a tube followed by a corresponding bumper of water so it would mix well in the stomach. The stomach eats all alone. Saves time.

But the assistant who watches over you has to be absolutely trustworthy. Who to ask?

My successor?

But he'd want to eliminate me; that's only human.

Ask nothing of anyone. Rest. You have the right.

I lock myself in the lab.

I develop M's photographs. The negatives would be enough, but why not do a little bit better?

Print them.

I can't imagine what anyone sees in these family photographs. The dead cousin of X's friend, who only visited once. Y (brother of Z)'s ex-fiancée, W's sister-in-law.

Children against a background of blue sky, diving.

A long and narrow footbridge. You can become engulfed in the water. You can bring back all the sounds; I know how to do it.

— *Let's go; dive!* cries the young woman in stripes. *Dive in! It's marvelous!*

Let's go, by God! cries M, his face all squished together under his bathing cap.

A series of swimming lessons. Photo 1. A belt hanging from a platform by a winch. Photo 2. The student is lowered into the water.

Next, they attach lead to the belt to force you to swim. They make it heavier and heavier to compensate for the progress. Photos 3 and 4.

— *Let 'er down,* says M. Photo 5.

I give the sign and George turns the handle. Photo 6. The little one is struggling. Photo 7. Two turns. She's under water. Photo 8. Three turns. You see the bubbles. They bring her back up. Photo 9. You have to increase it a little each time. George knows just how to regulate it. A little ecological electroshock. It helps. It's a lesson and a cure at the same time.

It's marvelous.

I see why it interests them. That doesn't mean I don't have to save her though.

4. Save her.

36

I'll tell her: it's D–day.

— *You can't see a thing in this tunnel*, she whispers crawling along.

It's to the right. No, it's to the left. Wait. I put dead foxes in the dead–end branches on purpose to fool the dogs. It's to the right now. Come this way, no, not that way.

— *B-b-b-u-u-u-u*, she squeals.

Hold your tongue, for God's sake. We're not far enough away yet. Why can't you understand what you're told? I feel her breath very close and the pulse beneath her skin.

We'll take a room in the first hotel we can find. Grey sheets, flowered bedspreads. Metal furniture.

Shower with non–skid surface. *Paaaass me the little green bag.*

She's in the shower, and I'm sitting on the bed silently crying.

— *Hand me a towel.*

I take the sawed–off Ithaca Mag 10 out of my bag and place a box of cartridges on the left pillow.

— *What are you doing?*

Wait till I come back. Don't open the door. If someone tries to break it down with a hatchet or battering ram, fire away.

I turn back and slip a couple of slow–combustion grenades under her elbow. I give a friendly wink.

— *What are these for?*

What the hell do you think, I scream, I'm getting you out of this dump! Who the hell do you think is going to get you out of this dump?!

— *Y-γ-γ-γou.*

All right then. Follow instructions. When you fire, wear this. I hand her my steel vest. You fire, see, bam–bam, and it recoils. Breaks your ribs. There, wear it.

— *What are you going to do?*

You've got something in there, don't you? I pat her just above the navel.

That's not quite it, though. Something's

not quite right. It's not real life. I feel like it's not my life I'm living. I don't have a life. It's not a life. I have no life.

It's not my life.

Anyway, eat. I take two tuna–fish sandwiches out of my bag. I'll be back.

37

We'll rent an apartment.

Sitting on a folding metal chair in front of the little window looking out into the court-yard. Sounds of breakfast + rattling dishes + competing radios pouring out the windows, linking the kitchens. Everything is in every-thing. It's marvelous. *I destroy bad memories.* Twin courtyards separated by a garden that joins twin buildings. Orange curtains, green lawn, yellow irises.

Here + never different + we here + beauti-ful day = ?

She's asleep.

I see what she's going to see later when she wakes up. I'm early.

I'll tell her that. It's luminous. When some-one doesn't sleep, he sees things first. Long before she does, I hear the sounds that will be slowly arriving at the other end of her dreams. It's extraordinary.

She's sleeping because she's bored. I'm not fun enough. That's it. That's my problem. Because I have to prepare our future life, D-day = zero.

We shouldn't have left. We should have stayed where we were. Old answers to new questions? Or old questions for new answers?

She doesn't know a thing. She's asleep. Are you sleeping?

I'm sorry I did it, you know.

— *I know.*

I don't have a house. Have you thought about that? Have you <u>really</u> thought about it?

— *Yes.*

Oh thank you, thank you so much. And again, bravo for the stuttering. It has such an air of authenticity.

— *I love you enormously.*

Me too.

— *Me too.*

You're my super-sister.

— *Thanks.*

Nonetheless, we should have stayed where we were. It's wrong to want to change.

I'd stand on a tree trunk and tell her:

Oh kiss me there
Oh kiss kiss me there

— It's the place you've told me about — is t-t-t-that it? With all the dead leaves all all all over the place. And then there's t-t-t-too much water everywhere. We'll d-d-d-drown.

It's winter now; just wait till you see it in the summer. In the summer, it's magnificent. Ah, (sigh) (sigh) in the summer. The sun reflecting off the water. Everything is in everything.

I do cartwheels around her. A–one and a–two and a–. Know that I tremble for you I tremble for you. Figuratively I tremble. Touch me there. Don't be shy.

I love to share my joy with you.

I run around in all directions to impress her.

We'll live quietly. What do you want for dinner? Rabbit? Coming right up. Bang–bang. The rabbit is on the fire, paws neatly tucked

up. House salad. Apple wine. Hand-dried to-
bacco. Hammock.

— *I want to go back n-n-n-now.*

Well, I'm not stopping you, no, no. I could
have tied you up, but no, nothing farther
from my thoughts. Go on then, you're perfectly free. Tie you up? Never.

— *T-t-t-tie m-m-me up?*

Never, never would I do such a thing. I'll
love you forever, <u>even in a city</u>. Anywhere at
all. I have an honest face. My words match
my tone. I talk neither too loudly nor too
much. No weird twitches or squints.

I'm well-adjusted.

You know, it's the first time I've ever seen
in color. It's extraordinary. It's thanks to you. I
flash a quick smile so she won't get nervous.
Everything's fine.

For a moment, nothing happens. Like it
should be done. Don't pressure her. Don't exaggerate.

No point in overdoing it.

I come up on her very quietly, still talking.
I decide to get smaller. Her suddenly-

longer legs extend the trunks of the poplars. On the other side of the wheat, the sex flat. Her hairs, immense. The feet, telescoped up to the head by perspective like those of our Lord on the dissection table in the image I store in my memory.

The one in the stained–glass window that I pass on my runs.

38

I'll go to a bar.

The girl behind the counter chirps *Hello*.

I walk out and then I go back in.

She saw me walk out and when I walk in again she says *hello* automatically. I walk out again and I come back in again, and she says *hello*, thinking I didn't hear her the first time.

I walk out and I come back in and I say hello, she says *hello* for the fourth time thinking that I've forgotten the previous ones.

I walk back out again and I come back in again and I say hello again, she replies *hello*, thinking I'm nuts. All five times in precisely the same way.

I elbow up to the bar and then I sense that something's not quite right.

1 square yard of lettuces destroyed
by a single mole
it's simple arithmetic

If there were more cows
there'd be no more hedges
if there were no more hedges
there'd be no more birds

If there were no more birds
there'd be no more hawks
if there were no more hawks
there'd be too many moles

The man who's talking turns and stares at me, though I can't think why. So far I've said nothing but hello. He keeps staring at me as he talks to make me nervous. I smile, thinking that'll ease the strain.

Wrong. He gets up and walks straight toward me.

Left hook, followed by a right swing with his whole body weight behind it right on the chin. Just as his knees are buckling, I catch him with a left into the kidneys: internal bleeding, etc.

There's an enormous barracuda looming over the bar, bizarrely naturalized as if painted in oils.

With the greasy steam from the croque-monsieur machine right below it?

Install a ventilator hood – a much more practical solution than washing it every day, and the ceiling's going to yellow anyway, despite all the cleaning.

Not that you'd notice it.

The way an electric floor waxer blocks up all the cracks in the parquet forever.

The bartender comes up. A beer – not too cold, I say. And I don't add "like it should be."

I see his left hand slide toward a hiding place under the bar that no doubt conceals a length of lead–filled plastic tubing.

I plant my knife so deeply into his right hand that I bury the blade in the wood beneath.

Before he can stop staring at the thing in astonishment, I'm over the bar and giving him a solid one to the base of his nose. I land on one foot and use the other to kick in the liver of the first customer to throw himself upon me.

The second gets a left with a definitive

twist at the end.

As for the third, who went for my neck, I tossed him over my shoulder. Sharp snap as spine meets concrete.

Unfortunately, the beer was a little cold. Seems the warm-beer tradition is disappearing. Along with recipes like beer soup – you just can't find them anymore. Oyster soup, too – who today knows how to make a top-notch oyster soup like in the old days?

They enter, white tablecloth and steaming Sheffield soup tureen. *Hellllo* what's this? Toss the hat onto the sideboard. Impeccable. Lift the lid, and there they are, floating barely cooked on top of the broth. A sprinkling of breadcrumbs and off we go.

All that – caput.

– *What do I care. I hate soup*, he says without looking at me.

Ok, I see. You have to humor children. It remains engraved like a punishment. You're not sick.

The memory of these traumas, I continue, having gotten his attention, besides, it's a relatively recent science, developed by the war industry (you only have to look at the trenchcoats, atomic electricity, crematoriums, vulcanized rubber soles), memory explains this rebellious behavior – not at all abnormal.

There's nothing wrong with you.

His two hands remain motionless on the bar, which could do with a bit of cleaning. I was going to tell him how you can turn a glove into a bar–rag but he swiveled on his stool and switched on an enormous radio above his head.

An unknown voice.

39

It could happen to anybody
the banks are a bit slippery

And just like that
drowned

Putrefied
the eyes

All beaten up
an arm missing
ripped off no doubt

By the force
of the current

The human being
can't stand
more than one dose of such

A lizard
has a different standard

Swimming
is primordial
I say

Today
we don't do the frog

It's right into the big pond
race you to the pole let's go

What did they do about the menhirs?
same thing
let's go

Today the human being
is less capable
of [ ]

Things are degenerating
it's clear

Same thing with swimming
they used to
really teach you

Now it's superficial
if not the two young guys wouldn't have drowned
it's perfectly clear

When you know you know
and not the other way around

Everything had been eaten
in little bits
the eyes

+ the putrefaction
so much for identification

+ all torn up by the rocks
and what with the silt and all

It's like peat
anything you bury in it
stays perfect

Like in a safe
not a wrinkle

40

I never should have left the knife.

Planted in his forehead. Clear proof. How stupid.

Do you know this knife?

No.

Then how come your name's engraved on the handle? Don't know.

Someone must have had it engraved, planning to give it to me as a present. But he didn't have time. That's it.

Lie detector + Truth serum = 20 years without the option.

I'm not a spy. I've never been a spy. And a knife can't prove that I was.

I scream, jumping up and pushing against the wall, which falls down.

But it doesn't fall down. There's no one here. Relax. Take a deep breath. It's ok. All right, it's ok, all right. I sleep badly. I'm slowing down, I've said so already. No use trying to hide it.

I've got to work out.

And if it was he?

The unknown guest?

The colonel?

But it was he. Ever since the beginning. And me, I didn't see a thing. Of that I'm sure. I passed him in the hallway, and he looked straight at me – then winked just after.

He winked at me.

That's the signal. Got to admit, I didn't catch on for a minute. What a pro.

I keep telling myself he must have been doing it from the start. Remarkable. A real artist. What a brilliant idea – to act like a total idiot. I'm going to tell him: bravo for that great move, telling all those stupid long-winded stories to allay their suspicions.

I go down the icy hallways as fast as possible in my felt shoes.

Knock–knock.

– *Come in.* He's awake.

– *Ah, thanks.* Taking the journal I hold out to him.

I've got them, Colonel.

– *What?*

Listen, I whisper, I've got to tell you, even if it's not my place (#1 obey without thinking of the consequences, even the absurd ones you can't help imagining, #2 professional secrecy, #3 disappear in case of failure at the target, #4 the utopia of work perfectly executed and without human resistance), I've got to warn you that those photos are of no interest whatsoever. Just personal stuff, family, vacations, etc.

No submarine plans. Just a bunch of people swimming, that's all. No information here.

This isn't the eagle's nest.

They've changed. They're no longer dangerous, no longer extremists. You've seen it for yourself.

Speaking of that, brilliant cover. Ingenious, that playing the utter idiot bit. Remarkable.

— *Such beautiful September light. But watch out nippy in the evenings. What they're saying about winter time is ridiculous. Better cover the dogs.*

Listen, there must be some mistake. I don't get the point, what's this mission all about? But what had to be done is done. No discussion. No one's seen anything. Even if I did go a little too far. But it's only normal to want to improve things. To want to adapt to local customs.

When in Rome, do like the Romans, I say louder so he'll hear me.

After so much listening at keyholes, you become a spy. Or else it's the other way around. It's the egg that makes the chicken. I laugh. It's too much.

He gives me a weird look.

I keep on thinking that there must be some mistake in our objectives. They must have gotten mixed up. Procedures got changed.

Unless there was a code. You put the first names of each one end to end going clockwise and – ! – you've got the word. H.E.L.P. That could be it. I'll have to check of course. But they've got guys in the lab to do all that. All's well that ends well.

He gives me an even weirder look.

That's it. I get it. He's acting like he knows nothing. He's a real pro. He's trying to tell me that the place is bugged.

And me, telling all.

— *Perhaps it's a good time to change them?*

The flowers. There's a microphone in the flowers. Not a bad idea. Except for the amplified breathing every time someone sticks his nose into them for a good whiff.

Very good, milord. I grab the flowers and trample them underfoot, making a sign in the air to show him I've understood. Shhh.

You've seen the team, I add, speaking low. I've trained them from the bottom up for D-day. Mentally superior. Third generation. They don't even know what they're doing but they'll do it all right. No questions asked. No more mission. Just pure work.

Or else he's trying to tell me I'm fired.

That's it. It's over. It could happen to anybody. Just because you're from the other side, they automatically think you're going to work for them anyway. They fire you with no warning, and you continue. You stay there forever not knowing that it's over. Useless night patrols. Throw away the plans. Too much gear. Voluntary exile. Forced celibacy.

Great body for nothing.

— *Bring me a plate of cold meat and pickles, please.*

The cold war, I understand, milord, I say out loud.

— *That's right. With pickles. And add a little hot water*, pointing to a bowl in which he's resting his feet as he opens the paper.

— *You like her, don't you, the little redhead,* he adds, pinning me with his eye, *a dangerous one, eh?* He winks + a little friendly hand signal bing bing two times with his index finger, thumb in the air like a little revolver = goodbye.

I understand. Good. A new mission.

Things don't stop just like that. They're satisfied with my work after all.

If I start something, I see it through to the end. I never forget my duty.

I did well not to escape with her.

She's not on our side.

It's perfectly clear. I understand it all. I almost fell into the trap.

Incredible.

41

Fifteen yards to the right.

Another 20 yards along the grass *this is the hard part, and then resurrection* leap the gate spring back flex the knees 25 yard run let's go not bad 2 yards/stride *even through the raids* 90 yards *straight into the big pond* 110 yards sun shadow sun shadow I've got to get in shape for the future.

350 yards *in the black pools in the black pools* 400 yards *Pegasus and the Unicorn* zzzip into the springy green 430 yards springy 2 yards 27/stride *there's always a high and a low* 470 yards green green of the turf on the track to the end 500 yards *planet Mars planet Mars* 600 yards I'm mad as a March hare but fast zzzip 800 yards go down to the left *Ah, if only we had a little more ether, Major* vertical tunnel trail new green life the true life *oh well we'll do it anyway.*

I remember everything.

Oh myyyyy luuuvly valentiiine I run I run

down into the vertical green tunnel my stomach in my heels the hooves of the flying stag muzzle plunged into the airy earth mud of me later on 1 mile *a little turn of the screw a little turn of the screw* red poppies pound pound pant pant 2 miles red red poppies green turf down low on the sides of the deep springy tunnel of the springy field 3.8 miles.

For a moment, nothing happens rest a few minutes it'll be all right breathe breathing normal.

The arms pumping in rhythm yes.

Hands outstretched, supple breathe in breathe out stretch the hands breathe in yes flex yes, eyes on the horizon yes.

I have my own language. I put the necessary words in the best possible order. There-the–grass–path line that guides me green.

The white wake of me who made it running.

I know where I'm going. I like what's happening. I am at my service and in the middle of doing it. I'm entirely at my service. Because I am multiple.

I am whole.

Said is as good as done.

I'm enshrined in my memory. Engraved into the landscape. I cut a line into the earth as I run. I am this line made by walking. I'm running in my stained–glass window. In the compartments of colors that simplify everything that exists.

Small against green background.

Red sky.

Yellow arms.

Blue feet.

Get a move on 22 yards/stride shortcut through the fields 4 miles hedge jump it I destroy bad memories rabbit's foot kangaroo of the outback hop 5 miles black jay cumulo–nimbus 6 miles *a sense of volume with the broom a huge family of broom* fly jump hop leg–snap rubble rust caterpillar compressed.

I remember everything. I replace all the words I said by others that are simpler. It equals everything equals I equal nothing.

Sheer bridge. I am there. A fish 1 pound 3 ounces doing a hand–stand on its back fin. A little blurry. Here and now. The green screen of it all braided together ouf ouf the minuscule green details which together make everything look green 7 miles run faster ouf ouf pure work pure work 8 miles *it's hard with a handicap like that* 9 miles *there's a carrot in the bullet hole* 12 miles three raw green grasshoppers behind a willow 15 miles *pull pull* soaring poplar with three black pigeons head thrown back summit zenith catapult to the sky a new lease a new life I know it all.

In the deep crack in the interior of the inside there where you see the little [ ] things *those you know like birds but they don't fly crumbled powdered cages in the air in the earth is that it?* Those [ ] those? the non-name? The little no-word things. Can I say that? Does it work? Is it valid?

† = the [ ] X ∞

Pegasus and the unicorn that's us 27 miles *oh oh he disappeared into the machine* in the deep trail trail trail into the forest I remember that my name is Rob son of Rob descendent robin ball-bearing no friction pure course pure work. Run through the garden of effort. The void before you as you run. Sucked up into the void like Peter Pan and his super-sister ffffffffffffffffffff. Sucked up into the excavated night. Void star. Exiled from the inside-out.

You're my super-sister.

March.

I'll be your bear.

And again, bravo for the stuttering.

Well done.

Jump' hedge' jump' hedge' *straight into the big pond* I destroy bad memories caterpillar of the fields *compressed come on it's great hurry come on it's not cold no come on* 40 miles *straight into the big pool* I am biodegradable.

I see in color inside the hole.

Me in three dimensions that move in slow motion. My heart buried. Memory self-dead. I run I know it all by heart I'm whole I blend into the set it's my turn 44 miles double oxer river I won't lower the bar *straight into the big pool* to become trees to become the trees to become a tree to become the tree.

42

What if I go in disguise?

Brilliant. Now that I know the whole story, I'll catch them out in no time.

I phone from inside the house feigning an exterior call.

Handkerchief over the mouthpiece. Hello my dear sir. Colonel +++++ here, I say in-audibly, sort of Roubonsoon, Rooobot'sson.

— *What?*

Rooo–booo–sooon, I say hyper–distinctly pinching my nose.

— *Excuse me but I can hardly hear you.*

I'm a friend of your friend Coudander-stam. Very fast.

— *Sorry, I didn't quite catch the name.*

Coudanderstam, I snap nasally and even faster.

— *Ah, yes, of course, yes certainly. Delighted.*

It just so happens that I'm in your area for a few days on maneuver. A real circus. We've got the guys from the 2nd Zouaves and the whole nine yards, helicopter, etc. A real thrill for the boys.

– *Fabulous. Can you come by for lunch?* responds the distant voice.

That'll be something.

– *What? I can't hear you very well.*

I said, With pleasure. I was just congratulating myself on the coincidence that made me choose to – how can I put it – carry out my patriotic duty in your neck of the woods.

Got to do what you can for a friend.

That reminds me of something a certain dictator said about us; he said something like, "They're a country of hicks who just could end up leading the fashion industry," and you know, he wasn't wrong, even if a few things have changed.

But not all that much, eh? That'd be something if things really had changed, eh? Things never change, eh? Re–arm 'em and send 'em back out.

I add a laugh at least a minute long to that one.

— Uh, yeah, right, I gotta say (…) It's true that, today, well (…)

No need to explain, I say cutting him off. Pray don't elaborate. Welcome a little calm eh? Feeling a bit overextended? Well, you should know the symptoms. Not exactly good timing, is it? In fact, pretty bad, given the circumstances.

Just when you need an eagle eye and a wolf's stride.

— Whaaaat?

The situation's bad really bad you need nerves of steel, eh?

— It's true, I admit (…) but let's not exaggerate. We say things sometimes that, well, how can I put it (…)

We'll have all the time we need to talk this thing over, and under the ideal conditions, won't we?

From what I hear you're very very well organized. Re-laugh. What time?

— One o'clock, says the farther–and–farther–away voice.

And I take it your daughter will be there?

— *My daughter?*

Yeah, the little redheaded number. I take it it's more than just a friendly understanding with the gardeners, eh? Ah, Nature. What time?

— *One o'clock* said the dimmer–and–dimmer voice.

Delighted, etc. Stuff cheeks with special gum. Dye hair with black wax. Glue on false badger–brush moustache. Tri–focal glasses with tinted contact lenses. Shoes done up in imitation ostrich–skin. Riding breeches. Hazelnut crop in hand. Sharp tweed jacket. Stolen white shirt.

Wake up early.

Rent a fast car.

Turn into the drive between the open gates.

Floor it, 7400 rpm.

Several miles through a tunnel of over–hanging elms.

Break out of the trees as you round a curve and suddenly glimpse a vast red brick facade bristling with chimneys. Plunge back into the dark tunnel of over–hanging trees.

Break out into the light.

Double clutch. Slight skid around in a 146 degree arc. No tracks left in the plush gravel.

Cut the engine.

Leap over the low door, legs first followed by the head levered by the arms. Hop. Twist of the hips, and land, both feet on the ground.

GREEN INTEGER
Pataphysics and Pedantry

Douglas Messerli, *Publisher*

Essays, Manifestos, Statements, Speeches, Maxims,
Epistles, Diaristic Notes, Narratives, Natural Histories,
Poems, Plays, Performances, Ramblings, Revelations
and all such ephemera as may appear necessary
to bring society into a slight tremolo of confusion
and fright at least.

MASTERWORKS OF FICTION

Masterworks of Fiction is a program of Green Integer to reprint important works of
fiction from all centuries. We make no claim to any superiority of these fictions
over others in either form or subject, but rather we contend that these works are
highly enjoyable to read and, more importantly, have challenged the ideas and
language of the times in which they were published, establishing themselves over
the years as among the outstanding works of their period. By republishing both
well known and lesser recognized titles in this series we hope to continue our mission of bringing our society into a slight tremolo of confusion and fright at least.

BOOKS IN THIS SERIES

Charles Dickens *A Christmas Carol* (1843)
Gérard de Nerval *Aurélia* (1855)
Thomas Mann *Six Early Stories* (1893–1908)
William Dean Howells *The Day of Their Wedding* (1895)
Arthur Schnitzler *Lieutenant Gustl* (1901)
Joseph Conrad *Heart of Darkness* (1902)
Gertrude Stein *Three Lives* (1909)
Knut Hamsun *A Wanderer Plays on Muted Strings* (1909)
Francis Carco *Sreetcorners* (1911–1912)
Knut Hamsun *The Last Joy* (1912)
Ford Madox Ford *The Good Soldier* (1915)
William Carlos Williams *The Great American Novel* (1923)
Arthur Schnitzler *Dream Story* (1926)

Anthony Powell *Venusberg* (1932)
Sigurd Hoel *Meeting at the Milestone* (1947)
Gertrude Stein *To Do: A Book of Alphabets and Birthdays* (1957)
Ole Sarvig *The Sea Below My Window* (1960)
José Donoso *Hell Has No Limits* (1966)
Yi Ch'ŏngjun *Your Paradise* (1976)
Raymond Federman *The Twofold Vibration* (1982)
Anthony Powell *O, How the Wheel Becomes It!* (1983)
Tereza Albues *Pedra Canga* (1987)
Toby Olson *Utah* (1987)
Thorvald Steen *Don Carlos and Giovanni* (1993/1995)
Jean Frémon *Island of the Dead* (1994)
Leslie Scalapino *Defoe* (1994)
Norberto Luis Romero *The Arrival of Autumn in Constantinople* (1995–1997)
Olivier Cadiot *Colonel Zoo* (1997)
Mohammed Dib *L. A. Trip: A Novel in Verse* (2003)

SELECTED OTHER TITLES [LISTED BY AUTHOR]

±Adonis *If Only the Sea Could Sleep: Love Poems* [1–931243–29–8] $11.95
Hans Christian Andersen *Travels* [1–55713–344–1] $12.95
Eleanor Antin [Yevegeny Antiov] *The Man Without a World: A Screenplay*
[1–892295–81–4] $10.95
Ingeborg Bachmann *Letters to Felician* [1–931243–16–6] $9.95
Krzysztof Kamil Baczyński *White Magic and Other Poems*
[1–931243–81–6] $12.95
†Henri Bergson *Laughter: An Essay on the Meaning of the Comic*
[1–899295–02–4] $11.95
Charles Bernstein *Republics of Reality: 1975–1995* [Sun & Moon Press:
1–55713–304–2] $14.95
Shadowtime [1–933382–00–7] $11.95
André Breton *Arcanum 17* [1–931243–27–1] $12.95
Earthlight [1–931243–27–1] $12.95
Lee Breuer *La Divina Caricatura* [1–931243–39–5] $14.95
Luis Buñuel *The Exterminating Angel* [1–931243–36–0] $11.95
Olivier Cadiot *Art Poetic'* [1–892295–22–9] $12.95

† Author winner of the Nobel Prize for Literature
± Author winner of the America Award for Literature
• Book translation winner of the PEN American Center Translation
  Award [PEN–West]
* Book translation winner of the PEN/Book-of-the-Month Club
  Translation Prize
+ Book translation winner of the PEN Award for Poetry in Translation